Ben's skin was smooth and warm, brute strength rippling beneath its surface.

In one bold, swift movement he pulled Callie's vest over her head, kissing her as if she was the one thing in the world that he truly possessed.

Right now she was. When his movements slowed, tender now, she began to tremble. His hand lingered for a moment over the catch at the back of her bra in an implied question, and Callie reached behind her, undoing it for him. She felt his lips curve into a smile against hers as he gently pulled the straps from her shoulders.

"Your skin… So soft…" His fingers were exploring her back, her breasts crushed against his chest. Callie moved against him, desperate for a little friction, groaning in frustrated impatience when it wasn't enough.

"Look sharp…" She whispered the words Ben called when he wanted to hurry the crew along, and he chuckled.

"Is this an emergency?"

"Yeah. I'm calling a Code Red…" She gasped into his ear, clinging to his shoulders.

Dear Reader,

Christmas is a little piece of magic. A few days when we can take some time out. Ben Matthews is a firefighter, and this year he's working over Christmas, but he's still determined to enjoy as much as he can of the celebrations.

Callie Walsh's childhood Christmases didn't contain much sparkle, and she can do without it now. When Ben shows her that it's not too late to feel the special magic of Christmas, they both believe that this can't last. When Christmas is over, they'll part and return to their everyday lives.

But things don't work out quite as they'd planned. Was their Christmas together just a bubble that will burst under the pressures of reality? Or can Ben and Callie recreate the magic next Christmas and make it permanent this time?

Thank you for reading Ben and Callie's story. I'm always thrilled to hear from readers, and you can contact me via my website, annieclaydon.com.

Annie x

FIREFIGHTER'S
CHRISTMAS BABY

———

ANNIE CLAYDON

HARLEQUIN® MEDICAL ROMANCE™

Recycling programs
for this product may
not exist in your area.

ISBN-13: 978-1-335-66385-6

Firefighter's Christmas Baby

First North American Publication 2018

Copyright © 2018 by Annie Claydon

Printed in U.S.A.

Books by Annie Claydon

Harlequin Medical Romance

Stranded in His Arms

Rescued by Dr. Rafe
Saved by the Single Dad

The Doctor She'd Never Forget
Discovering Dr. Riley
The Doctor's Diamond Proposal
English Rose for the Sicilian Doc
Saving Baby Amy
Forbidden Night with the Duke
Healed by the Single Dad Doc
From Doctor to Princess?

Visit the Author Profile page
at Harlequin.com for more titles.

To Sareeta. With grateful thanks
for steering me through my last four books
with such grace and aplomb.

CHAPTER ONE

AFTER TWO WEEKS of feeling the sun on his skin, and not having to bother with a razor, Ben Matthews had cut himself shaving. His uniform had felt unfamiliar and a little too crisp when he'd put it on this morning, but it was good to be back in a routine. The thing about holidays was that they gave him far too much time to think, and he was ready to get back to work now.

'Good holiday?' The fire station commander smiled across his desk, and Ben nodded.

'Has anything been happening here that I should know about?'

'I imagine you've already read the station reports?' Ben nodded in response. 'The only other thing is our visitor this morning.'

'Yes?' As the watch manager, Ben always liked to have a little warning if an inspection was taking place, but he had no concerns. It was a matter of both principle and pride that he and his crew were constantly ready for anything.

'She's a photographer. This is just a preliminary visit, she'll be back again in a month to take photographs over Christmas. It's partly her own project, to widen her portfolio, but we have an option to use any of the photographs she takes in our publicity campaigns and there's also going to be a calendar, which we'll be issuing at the end of next year.'

This all seemed very rushed. Ben wished he'd known about it when it had been in the planning stage, rather than being presented with a fait accompli. 'And this has all been agreed?'

'There wasn't much time to set it up. Ms Walsh specifically requested that she take the photographs over Christmas to add authenticity to the calendar shots. She's hoping to include some off-duty moments.'

Ben frowned. The only calendar he'd seen that had featured firefighters had involved underwear and Santa hats. And that was just the men...

'This is going to be...done sensitively, I imagine?'

'Of course. It's a bit of fun but there's a serious message, too. We want to raise public awareness about what we do, as well as raise money.'

'Right.' Ben was all for the serious message. Just as long as this photographer understood that too. 'The crew knows about this?'

'Yes, they're all for it. Ms Walsh came in last

week with her portfolio and showed us some of her work. I thought it was excellent, and there was some disappointment amongst the other crews when she chose to shadow Blue Watch.'

This photographer seemed to be calling all the shots. Not with *his* crew...

'And you've given her a free hand?'

The station commander smiled. 'I haven't imposed any restrictions on her, if that's what you mean. I know I can count on you to ensure the smooth running of the operation.'

'In that case...' Ben needed to get back to his crew. Now. Before this photographer started to think she *did* have a free hand and anyone persuaded anyone else that taking their shirts off was a good idea. 'I'll be getting on if there's nothing else.'

'No, nothing else.' The station commander picked up a file from his desk, and Ben rose, heading for the door.

Ben opened the door of the ready room and found it empty. Of course it was. Gleaming red and chrome was sure to appeal as the backdrop for the calendar photographs. Walking downstairs into the garage, he heard voices and laughter.

'No, I don't think that's going to work.' A woman's voice, clear and brimming with humour. 'I'm after something a bit more spontaneous...'

'*Spontaneous, my eye.*' Ben muttered the words to himself, marching through the narrow gap between the two fire engines and almost bumping into a woman who was standing by the front one of them.

At least she was good at getting out of the way. That was exactly the kind of aptitude she'd need. Ben caught a trace of her scent before she stepped quickly to one side and he came face to face with Eve and Pete, in full protective gear, standing beside the chrome fender, both with fixed smiles on their faces. That looked absolutely fine to him but, then, he wasn't in the business of art photography.

'Okay…let's break it up.' It seemed that the rest of the crew had decided that the taking of a few photographs required them to stand around watching. 'Give us a minute, will you?'

'Good to see you back, boss.' Eve grinned at him, taking her helmet off and unbuttoning her jacket. Ben heard the click of a camera shutter beside him and turned to the woman standing next to him as the crew dispersed quickly.

'Hi. I'm Callie Walsh.' She was holding the camera loosely in one hand, the other stretched out towards him. 'You must be Ben Matthews.'

'Yes.' Ben shook her hand briskly, omitting to say that he was pleased to meet her. 'The station commander told me you'd be here.'

She nodded, looking up at him. She had green eyes, the kind that seemed wholly dedicated to making a man stare into them, and the prettiest face he'd seen in a long while. The softness stopped there. Her short, corn-blonde hair was streaked with highlights and slicked back from her face. Spray-on jeans, a fitted leather jacket with more zips than seemed entirely necessary, and a look of determination on her face gave the overall impression of a woman who knew how to steamroller her way over pretty much anything.

Instinctively, Ben stepped back, leaning against the chrome on the front of the fire engine. When she raised her camera, pointing the bulky lens in his direction, he frowned.

'Before you take any more photographs, I think there are a few ground rules we need to have in place.'

'Of course.' Her face was impassive, and Ben wondered what she was thinking. That didn't matter. It didn't matter what he thought either. What mattered was the well-being and effectiveness of his crew.

'This is a working fire station…'

'I understand that. I know how to keep out of the way.'

That had only been his first concern. There were many more. 'As Watch Manager I'm responsible for the safety of everyone connected with Blue Watch…' His gaze drifted to the high heels of her boots. What she was wearing didn't come close to practical, if she was reckoning on venturing anywhere other than the ready room.

She seemed to read his thoughts. 'I'm hoping to just get everyone used to the idea of me being here today. I won't be accompanying you to any calls…'

'You won't be doing anything, at any time, unless I allow it.'

Perhaps he should qualify that. She could do whatever she liked, as long as she didn't mess with him or his crew. Callie was regarding him thoughtfully, as if she was assessing her next move.

'I can handle myself in emergency situations and I know how to follow operational and safety guidelines.' She unzipped her jacket, pulling a sheet of folded paper from an inside pocket. 'You probably haven't had a chance to look at my CV yet, but when you do you'll see that I'm a paramedic.'

If she'd been trying to surprise him, she'd pulled off a master stroke. When he took the paper, it seemed warm to the touch. Ben put that down to his imagination, rather than the heat of her body.

'When did you change jobs?' He unfolded the paper, scanning it.

'I didn't. I did an evening course in photography when I was at school and found that I can take a decent portrait. The income from that helped put me through my training as a paramedic, but now I want to extend my range a little. I think my first-hand experience of working with the emergency services gives me something unique to bring to this project.'

It was either a canny career move or some kind of personal crusade. It was difficult to tell what sparked the passion that shone in her eyes, and it really wasn't Ben's job to decide. All he needed to concern himself with was the practicalities, not whatever made Callie Walsh tick.

'All the same, I'd like to have first sight of all the photographs you take…'

Callie shook her head. 'That's not the way I work.'

'It's the way *I* intend to work.'

The edges of her mouth curved slightly, as if she already had her answer ready and had been waiting for the right time to slap him down.

'Then you'll have to adapt. I decide which of my photographs goes forward, and they go to the individuals concerned first, so they can review them and choose whether they want to sign a release. After that they go to the station commander. It's all agreed and I'm sure he'll show them to you if you ask nicely.'

Ben ignored the jibe. The procedure sounded reasonable enough but he would have no hesitation in circumnavigating it if he saw any threat to the welfare of the firefighters on his watch.

'All right. But if I feel that any of the photographs are inappropriate, I won't hesitate to block them.'

She folded her arms. 'You want to give me some artistic direction? What do you mean by "inappropriate"?'

He shouldn't feel embarrassed about this, even if her green eyes did seem to rob him of his capacity to stay dispassionate. It was simply an observation.

'I won't have any of my crew treated as…eye candy.'

Ben had expected she might protest. But her gaze travelled from his face, looking him up and down slowly. He tried to suppress the shiver that ran up his spine.

'You think you'd be good eye candy?'

Ben had a healthy regard for disdain, particularly when it emanated from a beautiful woman. It was almost refreshing.

'No, that's just my point.'

'Good. We're in agreement, then. Anything else?' Callie smiled. Her face became softer when she did that, and the temptation to enjoy this confrontation became almost overwhelming.

'Don't leave any of your equipment around. I don't want anyone tripping over anything.'

'I'm looking for spontaneity, not posed shots, and my camera is all I need. I never leave it around.'

'Okay. And if the alarm sounds, I need you out of the way. Quickly.'

'Understood. I'll flatten myself against the nearest wall.' Her gaze met his, and the thought of crowding her against a wall and kissing her burst into Ben's head. Maybe he'd muss her hair a little first and find out whether the soft centre that her lustrous eyes hinted at really did exist.

He dismissed the idea. If the alarm sounded, that would be the last thing he should be thinking about. And if it didn't then it was still the last thing he should be thinking about.

'That's great. Thank you.'

'My pleasure. May I get on and take a few shots now?'

'Yes, please do.' Ben turned, and walked away from her.

Maybe…

There was no maybe about it. Callie took his breath away. He'd aired his concerns less tactfully than usual because her mesmerising gaze had the power to make him forget all his reservations about her presence here. Even now, he was so preoccupied by the temptation to look back and catch another glimpse of her that he almost forgot he'd intended to go back his office and found himself heading on autopilot towards the ready room.

He didn't need this kind of complication. He'd been burned once, and if he allowed himself to be burned again, that would be entirely his fault. This was a professional relationship, and that was where it began and ended.

Callie watched his back as he walked away. Gorgeous. One hundred percent, knee-shakingly gorgeous. Dark, brooding looks, golden skin and bright blue eyes that the camera was sure to fall in love with. It was a shame about the attitude.

But he'd only said the things she'd known already. Stay out of the way. Treat the people she photographed with respect. Maybe he'd loosen up a bit when he saw that she knew how to handle herself.

Callie almost hoped that he wouldn't. If this guy ever actually got around to smiling at her, she'd be tempted to throw herself at him. If she wanted to avoid all the woman-traps that her mother had fallen into over the years, it would be a great deal easier if Ben Matthews didn't smile. Ever.

* * *

Ben had watched her all morning, and had hardly got a thing done. His crew, on the other hand, had been subtly persuaded to get on with their jobs, while Callie observed. She asked questions, laughed at everyone's jokes, and made a few self-deprecating ones of her own. It was all designed to put them at their ease, wipe the fixed smiles from their faces and get them to act naturally.

He saw her quietly lining up a few shots from the corner of the garage, and Ben had puzzled over why she should want them. Then the alarm sounded and she was suddenly back in that spot. He realised that it was the optimum out-of-the-way location to catch the movement of men and women, and then the noisy rush as the fire engine started up and swept out of the garage. She was good.

Maybe the professional thing to do was to try giving her the benefit of the doubt. He'd assumed that Callie was all about the cliché, but everything she'd done so far told him that she was all about the reality. Ben waited for a lull in the morning's activity and saw her heading for the ready room. He followed her, pouring himself a cup of coffee.

'Would you like one?' He gestured towards his own cup and Callie shot him a suspicious look. He probably deserved that.

'No, thanks. A glass of water…' She pursed her lips and something in her eyes told him that one of the quiet, dry jokes he'd heard her share with the crew was coming. 'If you trust me not to throw it all over you, that is.'

'You're thinking about it?'

'I'm told that wet fireman shots are very popular.' She smiled suddenly, and Ben reconsidered the dilemma that had been bugging him all morning. The best thing about Callie wasn't the way she moved, or her long legs, or even her bright green eyes. It was her smile.

'I guess I deserve that.'

'I guess you do.'

The sound of ice breaking crackled in his ears as he filled a glass from the water dispenser. Ben walked over to the table, leaving an empty seat between his and hers when he sat down.

Callie was watching him thoughtfully. 'Your concerns are reasonable. Everyone wonders what a photographer is going to make of them, and one of the issues that was raised when I visited last week was that I didn't glamorise your work.'

Ben had missed that. Maybe that was why his crew all seemed so relaxed around her. She'd already talked about the kind of photos she intended to take, and they knew what he hadn't stopped to find out. Perhaps he should try asking questions before he jumped to conclusions.

'Why did you choose Blue Watch?'

'Because you're the only ones on duty over the whole of the Christmas period.'

Of course. Ben felt suddenly foolish.

'If there's anything else you want to ask me...' Her gaze dropped from his face suddenly and she started to fiddle with her camera.

There was something. 'You say you're just an observer. But you frame your shots. I saw you scoping out the best place to stand when the alarm rang.'

This time she thought about her answer. 'Sometimes you have to be in the right place to see things clearly.'

Callie reached for the tablet on the table in front of her. Switching it on, she flipped through the photographs. 'What do you think of this one? Is it an accurate representation?'

Ben caught his breath. It wasn't just a photograph of a fire engine leaving the station, she'd caught the movement and urgency, hinting somehow at the noise and the touch of adrenaline that accompanied it. Ben hadn't thought that would be possible unless you'd lived those moments.

'That's really good.' *Really good* didn't sum it up. But, then, he was no art critic. 'I'd say it was accurate.'

'Thanks.' She stood up suddenly. 'I'd better get on.'

Ben watched her walk away from him. Perhaps *that* was the attraction. A beautiful woman who could walk away without looking back.

But maybe that was just the last eighteen months talking. He and Isabel had never really been right for each other, but he'd been intoxicated by her soft beauty. When he'd realised that it wasn't going to work between them, he'd tried to break things off gently, but Isabel wouldn't have it. Texts, phone calls. Looking out of his window to see her car parked outside at all hours of the day or night. And then the *real* craziness had started…

That was over now, and he didn't want to think about it. He wasn't particularly proud of the way he'd handled things and Isabel hadn't contacted him in months. A woman walking away from him was just that—not some sign that there was someone out there who could make him feel the things that had come so easily before he'd met Isabel.

He studiously ignored Callie for the rest of the day. She was making a good job of keeping out of the way, and that suited Ben just fine.

CHAPTER TWO

'THE PHOTOGRAPHS ARE IN, BOSS.' Ben found Eve hovering at the door of his office.

'Photographs?' He wondered whether his expression of surprise cut any ice. He'd been thinking about Callie a lot more than was strictly necessary over the last two weeks.

Eve rolled her eyes. 'There's a parcel on your desk. It came by courier.'

'Okay, thanks.' It seemed that Eve wasn't going to leave him alone to open it. 'Let's take a look then.'

Eve followed him into his office, looking over his shoulder as Ben carefully ran a knife around the tape that bound the box on his desk. Inside was a brief letter from Callie, stating that she'd enclosed a few photographs for review. And underneath that a stack of sealed manila envelopes, each of which carried a name and a *Private and Confidential* sticker.

'Where are mine…?'

'Hold on a minute.' Ben sorted through the envelopes, handing over the one that bore Eve's name.

'You can show them to me…if you want to.'

Eve was the one member of his crew that he wanted most to protect. Ben hadn't been there when she'd sustained the burns on her shoulder, but he'd been told how much courage she'd shown that day. And he'd seen the pain in her face when he'd visited her at the hospital. Eve had cried, just the once, saying that the burns were so ugly, and when she'd finally returned to work, Ben had noticed that she never wore anything that exposed her upper arms, even on the hottest day.

'I might…' Eve sat down on the chair next to his desk, running her finger under the seal of the envelope and taking the A4 photographs out. She flipped through them carefully and Ben saw her cheeks burn red. Then a tear rolled down her cheek.

If Callie had upset Eve in any way, if she'd made her feel anything less than beautiful, she wouldn't be coming back here. No more photographs, no more talking to his crew to gain their trust.

'What's up, Eve?' He tried to banish the anger from his voice, speaking as gently and quietly as he could. Eve tipped her face up towards him and suddenly smiled.

'Look at me, boss.'

As she handed the photos over, her hand shook. Ben took them, forcing himself to look.

There was one of Eve running, buttoning up her jacket as she went. Another of her climbing into the cabin of the fire engine. Eve's frame seemed somehow diminutive next to her crew-mates, but she was clearly one of a team and the angle from which the photographs had been shot showed her ahead of the men, not follow-ing on behind.

'These are... Do you like them?' Maybe Eve saw something in them that he didn't.

'Yes, I like them. I *really* like them.'

'Me too.' Ben looked at the next photograph, and saw what had prompted Eve's tears.

'Callie took this at your home?'

'Yes, we made an arrangement for her to come and see me. What...do you think?' Eve wiped the tears from her face with her sleeve.

She was sitting on the floor with her four-year-old son in her lap. Isaac was clutching a toy fire engine and Eve's dark hair was styled softly around her face. She was wearing a sleeve-less summer dress that showed the scars on her shoulder.

'I think... It's a lovely photograph of you and

Isaac.' Ben decided to concentrate on the mother and son aspect, and the love that shone in Eve's face.

'It is, isn't it? I didn't think…' Eve shrugged.

'Didn't think what?' Ben was still ready to spring to Eve's defence, but perhaps he didn't need to. Maybe she saw what he did, and that was what her tears were all about.

'I didn't think I'd ever wear that dress again. Callie and I talked about it for a while, she said that we could stop if I felt uncomfortable and that these photos were just for me, not anyone else.'

'You should be proud of yourself, Eve.' Somehow Callie had captured everything in the image. Eve's love for her son, her strength and her vulnerability. The scars looked like badges of courage and they brought a lump to Ben's throat.

'Yes.' Eve took the photographs back, hugging them to her chest as if they were something precious. 'I'm going to show the guys.'

Ben put his own envelope to one side, slightly surprised that there was one, and stacked the rest back into the box. 'Will you take these out with you? Make sure everyone gets just their own envelope.'

'Yep.' Eve paused, grinning. 'So you're not going to show me yours?'

His could hardly be as moving, or mean so

much. He tore at the envelope, taking out the glossy prints.

'Go on. Take a look.' He handed them straight over to Eve. He didn't much want to look himself, and find out how Callie saw him.

'Nice... Very action hero.' Eve laid the first photo down on his desk and Ben saw himself caught in the act of loading equipment onto the fire engine. A second showed him climbing into the cabin.

There was one more to go. And Eve was grinning suddenly.

'Wow, boss. Never knew you were a pin-up.'

'Neither did I.' Ben reached for the photograph, snatching it from her.

Oh. He remembered that now. He'd been sitting in the ready room, after returning from the fire they'd been called to that afternoon. Watching as Callie had talked to a couple of the other firefighters. Suddenly she'd turned and pointed the camera at him.

Perhaps it was Ben's imagination, but he thought he saw the subtle winding-down process after a call where there had been no casualties and the fire had been successfully contained. And there was something else. His eyes looked almost startlingly blue under tousled hair that was still wet from the shower.

'Do I really look like that?' For the first time

in his life it occurred to Ben that he looked handsome.

'Yeah, on a good day. Sometimes you look a bit rough…' Eve laughed at his protests, narrowing her eyes to squint at the photograph. 'Maybe she's turned up the blue tones a bit. She explained to me how you do that. She said that she could turn down the red of my scars a bit but when we'd talked about it I decided that she shouldn't. All or nothing, eh?'

'Good decision. You can be very proud of your photos, Eve.' Ben looked at his own photograph again. None of the other blues seemed to be so prominent. Maybe it was a trick of the light…

He decided not to think about it. Gathering up the photographs, he put them back into the envelope and threw it back into the box.

'Here. If anyone wants to see these, you can show them.' He led by example. If anyone on the crew wanted to see what Callie had made of him, they could have a good laugh over it.

'Right, boss. Thanks.' Eve put her envelope in the box with his and shot him a grin before she left him alone.

What Callie had made of him. It was a thought that wouldn't go away, because the photograph had hinted at the smouldering heat that invaded his thoughts whenever he looked at her.

He shook the thoughts from his head. Christ-

mas was only a week away and Callie would
be back to take the photos for the calendar. He
would be sure to thank her for her sensitivity
with Eve and then he'd keep his distance. Ben
didn't trust himself to do anything else.

Callie had stared at Ben's photograph for a long
time before deciding to include it in his envelope. Perhaps it looked a like a come-on, betray-
ing the way she saw him a little too clearly. But
it was really just the way that the lens saw him.
The camera was indifferent to him and incapable of lying. That image was all about Ben and
nothing about her.

Her friends would have taken one look at the
picture and told her that capturing Ben's smile
for real should be her number one priority over
Christmas. But anyone who seriously thought
she'd take that advice didn't know much about
her. Callie was all about avoiding risk.

It was one of the reasons she'd wanted this job
so much. She'd wanted to understand what made
the firefighters tick, what allowed them to do a
dangerous job and then go home to their families
afterwards. She'd been too young to understand
when her father had failed to come home from
work one day, but she'd understood her mother's
tears and in time she'd come to understand that
he'd never be coming home.

She'd learned afterwards that her father had been a hero. A police officer, called to an armed robbery that had gone bad. He'd saved two of his fellow officers but he had been unable to save his own wife and child from the mistakes and hardships that had resulted from his death.

It was the best reason in the world not to get involved with Ben, a man who took risks for a living, like her father had. He might be mouth-wateringly handsome and Callie had always had a soft spot for men with a hard exterior and warm eyes. But he was very definitely on her not-to-do list this Christmas. It was okay for the camera to register his smouldering eyes but she wasn't going to think about them.

One of the firefighters let her into the station on a crisp, cold Christmas Eve morning. Callie made her way to the ready room, adding the two dozen mince pies she'd made last night to the pile of boxes of Christmas fare in the kitchenette. Then she sat down, her camera ready, waiting for something to happen.

No sprayed-on jeans this morning. If he'd known in advance, Ben might have thought that Callie in a pair of serviceable trousers, heavy boots and a thick red hoodie would be an easier prospect. But that would have been a mistake because she still looked quite terrifyingly gorgeous.

He'd made sure that the photo of himself, captioned 'Hunk of the Month', had been taken down from the ready room notice-board. Everyone had taken their chance to have a good laugh, and there was no need for Callie to see it.

She was sitting quietly in the ready room. Blending in, as he'd seen her do before. Watchful, observing everything. He'd bet the silver sixpence from the Christmas pudding that she'd already sized up the decorations and the small tree in the corner of the room, deciding how best they might be put to use in her photographs.

'You're here.' He suddenly couldn't think of anything else to say.

'Yes.' She turned her green eyes up towards him thoughtfully. 'So are you.'

That got the patently obvious out of the way. Ben sat down.

'Eve showed me her pictures.'

She reddened a little, seeming to know exactly which of the pictures he was referring to. 'You know that she called the shots?'

'Yes, Eve told me that you'd talked about it all at some length, and that she was happy with what you'd done.' Ben liked it that Callie was unsure what his reaction might be, and that she actually seemed to care what it was.

She nodded slowly, obviously pleased. 'She

rang me and said she'd be happy for them to be included in the pictures for the calendar.'

'And what do you think?'

'I think they're exactly the kind of thing we want. But I'm going to leave it until after Christmas and give Eve some time to think about it. Sometimes people say yes to a proposal and then change their minds when it becomes a reality.'

'I'll leave you to sort that out with her.' Two weeks ago it had been unthinkable that he could leave Callie to negotiate directly with his team, but now... Maybe her photographs had worked a little magic on him as well.

'You're expecting to be busy today?' She asked the question with an air of innocence and Ben smiled.

'Yes, we're often busy over Christmas.'

'I'm hoping that you'll agree to my going with the crew on a call-out. The station commander gave me the go-ahead and I've signed the waiver. But the final decision's down to you.'

He'd been half expecting this. For someone who was so invested in how things looked, it was impossible that her own appearance didn't mean something. She'd even ditched the bulky camera, replacing it with a smaller one that might easily be stowed away inside a jacket.

'Can you earn it?' The words slipped out before he could stop them. He usually put things a little more tactfully than that, wrapping it all up in talk about basic fitness and health and safety procedures.

If it was the little tilt of her chin that he'd wanted to see, she didn't disappoint him. Neither did the defiance in her eyes.

'Just watch me.'

CHAPTER THREE

CALLIE WOULD HAVE thought that four years working as a first response paramedic might have allowed some of the more basic procedures to go without saying. But it appeared that Ben took nothing for granted.

'Don't forget to stand where he tells you.' Eve's eyes flashed with humour as she whispered the words to Callie.

'Sorry about this...' The yard wasn't the place to be in this freezing weather, and everyone looked as if they'd rather be in the ready room, making inroads into the stack of Christmas food.

Eve grinned. 'It's not you. He does it with everyone. Everyone he likes, that is...'

Right. This was obviously the hurdle that she had to jump to gain entry to the team. She could respect that, there was no such thing as being too careful when your job involved the kinds of risks that the crew faced every day.

'Callie! Over there...' Ben shouted, and she

started. She was already standing well out of the way of the fire crew, and the point he'd indicated precluded any good photographic shots of the imaginary conflagration.

She ran obediently to her allotted spot and he nodded, seeming to be fighting back a grin. 'All right. Thanks, everyone.'

The crew followed his lead, at ease now as they left their positions and started to meander back inside. Ben was suddenly one of them again, just another member of the crew, but Callie was under no illusions that as soon as the alert bell rang, he'd be their leader again.

'Did I pass?' She murmured the words to him as he strolled back across the yard towards her.

'Yeah. Full marks.' This time he allowed himself to smile. 'Make sure you do the same when this is for real.'

This wasn't for real? Full marks meant that she had a chance of going with the crew on their next call-out. That made it real enough.

They didn't have long to wait. When the alarm sounded, Callie was on her feet with the others, pulling on the high-vis protective jacket with 'Observer' written across the back of it.

She was familiar with the sound of a siren but it usually emanated from her own rapid response vehicle. The fire engine made more noise and she wasn't used to the sway of the vehicle or to being squashed between Eve and one of the other firefighters while someone else did the driving. Neither was she accustomed to feeling like a parcel, only there for the ride.

But she did as she'd been told, waiting for the firefighters to get out of the vehicle before she did. Smoke and flame plumed upwards from what looked like a storage yard behind a brick wall.

'Callie, stay right back. There are gas canisters in there.' There was a popping sound as one of the canisters exploded in the heat of the conflagration. Ben didn't look back to make sure that she complied with the instruction as he hurried towards the back of the fire truck, where the crew was already deploying two long hoses.

Water played over the top of the wall, another jet aimed at a gate to one side. Callie knew that the angles were carefully chosen to maximise the effect of the hoses, but it seemed that no one had actually made that decision. It was just a team, working together apparently seamlessly.

Photographs. That was what she was here for. She'd almost forgotten the camera in her hand in favour of watching Ben. In charge, ever watchful and yet allowing his crew to do their jobs without unnecessary orders from him. It was a kind of trust that she wished he might bestow on her.

He turned, waving her further back, pointing

to a spot beside the police cordon. At least she was out of his line of sight now, and she could remove the heavy gloves that made it practically impossible to take photographs. Not that it mattered all that much. She was standing so far back that the people behind the cordon probably had as good a chance of taking a meaningful shot as she did.

I hate this. She was used to working on her own and making her own decisions. But if she proved she could comply with Ben's orders, he might ease up on her a bit.

In the meantime, she'd do what she could. Callie turned for a shot of the cordon, people lined up behind it watching anxiously. Some were passers-by who'd stopped, while others in bright-coloured sweaters and dresses rather than coats had obviously been evacuated from the houses closest to the blaze. Over the steady thrum of the fire engine and the roar of the flames she could hear a child crying and another babbling in excitement.

Panning back towards the firefighters, a movement caught her eye. A twitch of the curtains in one of the houses in the row next to the yard. When Callie pressed the zoom, she saw a head at the front window.

'Ben…!' She ran towards the fire engine, screaming above the noise, and he glanced back towards her. 'Over there, look.' She pointed to the window and he turned suddenly, making for the house. He'd seen what she had, that the police evacuation had left someone behind.

It appeared that since he'd given Callie no indication that she should move, he expected her to stay where she was. Forget that. Callie tucked the camera into her jacket and followed Ben.

'Go back. We've got it…' They met on the doorstep. The woman had disappeared from the window and without a second glance at Callie he bent down, flipping open the letterbox to look through it and then calling out.

'That's right, my love. Open the door. No… No, don't sit down. You need to open the door for me.'

Suddenly he puffed out a breath and straightened, turning to Eve, who had arrived at his side. 'We have an elderly woman sitting on the floor, leaning against the front door. We'll go in through the window.'

Eve nodded and Ben reached into his pocket, pulling out a window punch. It took one practised movement to break one of the small glass panes in the windows at the front of the house.

'Callie, I won't say it again. You're in the way…' He didn't look round as he reached in, slipping the catch and swinging the window open.

'Since when was a paramedic *in the way* when

you have a possible trauma? You should be getting out of *my* way.' Callie resisted the temptation to kick him. Playing along with Ben at the fire station was one thing, but this wasn't the time or the place.

He turned quickly, a look of shock on his face. Then he took the helmet from Callie's hand, securing the strap under her chin and snapping down the visor. 'Put your gloves on. Stay behind me at all times. Eve, stay here and let me know if the fire looks as if it's coming our way.'

He pushed the net curtains to one side and climbed in, turning to help Callie through the window. She ignored his outstretched hand and followed him. When he led the way through to the hallway, Callie saw an elderly woman sitting on the floor behind the door. Her eyes were closed but her head was upright so she was probably conscious. Callie tapped Ben's arm to get his attention.

'Did she fall?'

'I don't think so. She just seemed to slide down the wall.'

'Okay.' Standing back wasn't an option now and neither was staying behind him. The house wasn't on fire and Ben's skills were of secondary use to her. Callie pushed past him and knelt down beside the woman, taking off her helmet and gloves. She wasn't used to working with these kinds of constrictions.

'Hi, I'm Callie, I'm a paramedic from the London Ambulance Service.'

The woman looked up at her with placid blue eyes. It seemed that the urgency of the situation had escaped her, and Callie saw a hearing aid, caught in the white hair that wisped around her face, with the ear mould hanging loose. She was clutching a pair of glasses that looked so grimy that they could only serve to obscure her sight.

Great. No wonder she hadn't responded when Ben had called through the letter box. Callie gently disentangled the hearing aid, putting it in her pocket. There was no time now to do anything other than make do with what the woman could hear and see.

'Are you hurt?' She tipped the woman's face around, speaking clearly.

'No, dear.'

'Have you fallen?'

The woman stared at her, her hand fluttering to her chest. Callie heard Ben close the sitting-room door so that more smoke didn't blow through the house from the broken window. The smell of burning was everywhere, filtering through every tiny opening from the outside, and Callie knew that the air quality in here wasn't good.

She felt a light touch on her shoulder. 'You're happy to move her?'

Suddenly Ben was deferring to her. Callie's quick examination had shown no sign of injury and the woman's debility and confusion might well be as a result of smoke inhalation. On balance, the first priority was to get her into the fresh air.

'Yes.'

Thankfully, he didn't waste any time questioning her decision. Ben used his shortwave radio to check with Eve that their exit was still clear and helped Callie get the woman to her feet. Her legs were jerking unsteadily and it was clear that she couldn't walk.

'Can you take her?' She'd be safe in Ben's strong arms. He nodded, lifting the woman carefully, and Callie scooted out of the way, opening the front door.

Outside, the fire in the yard was almost out, quantities of black smoke replacing the flames. Ben didn't slacken his pace until he'd reached the cordon, and as a police officer shepherded them through, a woman ran up to them.

'Mae… Mae, it's Elaine. Elaine Jacobs…' The older woman didn't respond, and the younger one turned to Ben. 'Bring her to my house. Over there…'

'Thanks.' Ben shot a glance at Callie and she

nodded. There was nowhere else other than the police car to set Mae down and examine her.

Ben carefully carried his precious burden into the small, neat sitting room, and Mrs Jacobs motioned him towards a long sofa that stretched almost the length of one wall. He put Mae down carefully and turned to Callie.

'Ambulance?'

'Yes, thanks.'

'Okay, I'll see to it.' He turned to Mae, giving her a smile, and her gaze followed him out of the room.

'I'm all right.' Mae seemed to be addressing no one in particular, and Callie guessed that she was trying to reassure herself as much as anyone else. She touched her hand to catch her attention.

'I know you are. Just let me make sure, eh?'

CHAPTER FOUR

HOWEVER HARD HE tried to put Callie into a box, she just seemed to spring straight out again. He'd thought her capable of steamrolling over him and his crew if he allowed her to, and then she'd shown herself to be sensitive enough to make a difference to the way Eve saw herself. Ben had tried to limit her to the role of observer, and she'd shown him that she wasn't just that either.

Perhaps he had trust issues. It made no difference what Callie did, he couldn't bring himself to trust the warmth that her mere presence sparked in his chest. Maybe he never would truly trust a woman that he was attracted to ever again.

When he knocked on Mrs Jacobs's front door, he meant to stay on the doorstep, but she wouldn't have any of it, ushering him inside and telling him that he couldn't possibly compete with the mess that her two teenagers were capable of making. Callie was kneeling beside Mae, chatting to her, and looked up when he entered the sitting room.

'Everything all right?'

'Yes. The fire's out and we're making everything safe.' He trusted his crew. He'd trusted Callie, back at the house, when she'd snapped suddenly into the role of paramedic. Maybe that was what he should remember, rather than the way her smile seemed to plunge his whole world into chaos.

'The ambulance is on its way?'

'Yes.'

Mae had turned her gaze up toward them, obviously following their conversation. By the simple expediency of cleaning her glasses and making sure that her hearing aids were seated correctly, Callie had wrought an amazing change in the elderly lady. Ben bent down, smiling at Mae.

'How are you feeling now?'

'Callie says I have to go to the hospital…' Her voice was cracked and hoarse, but it was difficult to tell whether that was the effect of emotion or smoke inhalation. 'On Christmas Eve…'

'It's best to be on the safe side. If it were me, I'd take her advice.'

He heard a sharp intake of breath behind him. Mae's presence in the room had probably saved him from the humiliation of one of Callie's put-downs.

Mae's questioning gaze focussed somewhere to his left, and he turned. Callie's smile was almost certainly for Mae's benefit, but still it made Ben's heart thump.

'I'll come to the hospital with you, Mae. We'll find ourselves a handsome doctor in a Santa hat, eh?'

'Thank you dear. You're very kind.' Mae managed a smile. 'I'll pick a nice doctor for you.'

Callie chuckled. 'Make sure you do. I don't want just any old one.'

He couldn't do anything to help with the journey to the hospital but he could make things a bit better for Mae's return. 'I know someone who'll board up the window for you. I'll write their number down…'

Mrs Jacobs rummaged in a drawer and produced a pen and paper. Ben scribbled the number on it and handed it to Callie. 'Tell them I gave you their details. They'll liaise with the insurance company and help get things moving.'

Mae shot him a worried look. 'How much will it cost?'

'It won't cost you anything. All part of the service, Mae.' It wasn't officially part of the service. The number was for a local charity. It had been Ben's idea to contact them and set up a task force to help vulnerable people clean up after a fire, and he and a number of the station staff volunteered with them.

'And when you get back from the hospital, you'll stay here over Christmas.' Mrs Jacobs sat down on the sofa next to Mae. 'No arguments, now. Stan and the boys will go over to your place and help sort things out there.'

'But…it's Christmas.' Despite her neighbour's firm tone, Mae argued anyway.

'Exactly. It'll do them good to go and do something, instead of sitting around watching TV and eating. I'm sure Stan's put on a couple of pounds already so he can do with the exercise.'

'You're very kind.' A tear dribbled down Mae's cheek. 'All of you.'

'It's Christmas. We'll all pull together, eh?' Mrs Jacobs put her arm around Mae and the old lady smiled, nodding quietly.

Ben beckoned to Callie and she frowned. He glared back, beckoning again more forcefully, and she rolled her eyes and followed him into the hallway.

'What? I'm busy.'

The tight-lipped implication that she was just trying to do her job and that he was getting in the way wasn't lost on Ben.

'I just wanted to know… How *is* Mae? Really?'

Callie's angry glare softened slightly and she

puffed out a breath. 'I've checked her over the best I can, and she doesn't seem to be having any difficulty with her breathing. But she has a headache and she seemed very confused earlier, and you can hear she's a bit hoarse. She needs to be seen by a doctor. I'm going to stay with her.'

The thought that Callie might not come back to the fire station once she had finished here filled Ben with unexpected dismay. He had no one but himself to blame if she made that decision.

'I shouldn't have said that you were in the way earlier. It won't happen again.'

'I can take care of myself in these situations. I do it all the time.'

'Got it. I apologise.' Ben saw her eyebrows shoot up in surprise. Was that what she thought of him? He was perfectly capable of saying sorry when the situation warranted it.

But prolonging the conversation now while she was still angry with him probably wasn't a good idea. He'd said his piece and he should go.

'I'll see you later?' Ben tried not to make a question out of it, but his own doubts leaked through into his words. Callie gave a nod and he turned, making for the front door. He guessed he'd just have to wait and see about that.

* * *

The wait at the hospital hadn't been too pro-tracted, and after X-rays and lung capacity tests had been carried out, Mae was discharged. They arrived back at Mrs Jacobs's house to find that the charity task force that Ben had put her in touch with had already boarded up Mae's win-dow.

She had no qualms about leaving Mae here. Two cups of tea and a plate of mince pies ap-peared, and a yelled exhortation brought Mrs Jacobs's son tumbling down the stairs, a board game in his hand. He and Mae began to sort through the pieces together, and Mae finally smiled.

Mae's Christmas would be just fine. Callie's was a little more uncertain. The success of her project at the fire station depended on clearing the air with Ben, and there was no time to sit quietly and wait for him to let her in. She had to do something.

She took a taxi back to the fire station. He wasn't with the others in the ready room and Cal-lie found him alone in the small office with the door wide open. She tapped on the doorframe and he looked up.

Blue eyes. The most photogenic eyes she'd ever seen, flickering with warmth and the hint of steel. The kind of eyes that the camera loved and… That was all. The camera loved them but Callie was just an impartial observer.

'Everything okay?'

'Yes. Mae was discharged from the hospital and she'll be staying with Mrs Jacobs over Christmas. The charity task force has been great.'

'Good.' His gaze was fixed on her face. 'I've been thinking about what you might be wanting to say to me.'

Perhaps he was trying out a management technique. Put yourself in the other person's shoes. Callie sat down.

'Okay, I'll play. What might I be wanting to say to you?'

'That I'm not giving you credit for the experience that you have. You need access to be able to work and I'm being unreasonable in withholding it.'

Actually, that pretty much summed it up. Callie dismissed the rather queasy feeling that accompanied the idea that he'd been reading her thoughts.

'And… I guess that you'd say in return that you and the others rely on teamwork. That kind of trust isn't made over a matter of days and you're not sure of me yet.'

The look on Ben's face told her that she was right. More than that, he found it just as disconcerting as she did to hear someone else voice his thoughts.

'I'll…um… I'll be honest. I wasn't much in favour of you being here when the station commander first told me about it.'

'Really? You hid that well.' Callie risked a joke. Somehow she knew that he wouldn't take it the wrong way.

He narrowed his eyes. Maybe he *was* taking it the wrong way. Then suddenly Ben smiled. 'So we see eye to eye, then.'

Rather too much so. If he really could see what was going on in her head… Callie gulped down the sudden feeling of panic. Of course he couldn't.

The awkward silence was broken by the alarm bell. Ben rose from his seat, making hurriedly for the door, and Callie followed him.

She took her turn climbing up into the fire engine and found Ben sitting opposite her. As the sirens went on and they started to move out of the fire station, he leaned forward, bracing his foot against the lurching of the vehicle and checking her helmet.

Callie frowned. He'd been the one to say it and he hadn't even listened to himself. He was still double-checking everything she did.

'If I get the chance, I'll take you in as close as

I think we can safely go.' The light in his blue eyes kindled suddenly.

'Thanks for that, boss.'

Ben's eyebrows shot up as he realised that Callie was using the word 'boss' to make a point. Then he grinned. Maybe this *was* going to work after all.

The word 'boss' on Callie's lips could hardly be anything other than a challenge. But they'd both risen to it. Ben had motioned her to stand next to him as he directed the firefighters in extinguishing a small blaze at the back of a shop. Callie had become like a shadow, never giving him a moment's concern for her safety, and adroitly stepping out of the way of both equipment and firefighters.

'I got some good shots. They'll do you all justice.' She waited until he was about to tell her that they were leaving now, catching his attention for the first time since they'd been there.

'Good. Thank you.' He smiled, and she smiled back. Then she turned to join the rest of the crew climbing back into the fire engine, leaving Ben with the distinct impression that his legs were about to give way under him.

It took some time to persuade himself that this evening would be nothing to do with wanting to spend more time with Callie but simply a matter of showing her another side of the job. But for once she made things easy for him. As the night shift arrived she hung back in the ready room, flipping almost disinterestedly through the photos she'd taken that day, as if she were waiting for something.

Ben dismissed the thought that it might be him. But then he found himself caught in her clear gaze.

'I wanted to catch you before I left. To say thank you for this afternoon.'

'My pleasure. You have plans for tonight?' Ben tried to make the question sound innocent. He'd already heard Callie's answer when Eve had asked earlier.

'No, not really. It's an hour's drive home and I'll probably just curl up with some hot soup and decide what I want to try and shoot tomorrow. You?'

'I'm going carol singing. We have a decommissioned fire engine, which is kept at one of the other stations. It's used for charity and public awareness events and this evening it's parked up in town. You should join me.'

She gave a little shake of her head. 'Are you ever entirely off duty?'

These days…no. Ben had always been immersed in his job but he'd known where to draw the line between work and home. But in the last year his work had been a welcome relief from worrying about what Isabel might do next.

He reached inside his jacket, laying two hats on the table. 'Can't really be *on* duty when you're wearing one of these.'

Callie's hand drifted forward, her fingers brushing the white 'fur' around the edge of the Santa hat and then moving to the bells around the edge of the green elf hat. A sudden vision of texture and movement and the feel of Callie's fingers on his skin drifted into his head. He could tell she was tempted to accept his offer.

'You get to pick. Elf or Santa.'

She smiled. 'I'll be Santa.'

Of course she would. He was beginning to understand that this was something they shared, and that she too never felt entirely comfortable unless she was holding the reins.

'Okay.' He handed her the Santa hat. 'Play your cards right and you might get to drive the sleigh.'

Green suited Ben. No doubt red would have done too, but Callie had to admit that he made a very handsome elf. No doubt he'd be the one who got presents wrapped twice as fast, without even breaking a sweat.

After the bustle of the fire station and the cheery goodbyes of the crew she'd suddenly felt very alone. She'd had to remind herself that returning to her cold, dark flat was exactly the way she wanted it. No one to welcome her home meant that there was no one to pull the carpet out from under her feet.

She pulled on a down gilet for warmth and put on her coat and gloves, attaching her camera to a lanyard around her neck, ready for use. Tonight was about photos and not Christmas cheer, she told herself stubbornly.

The quickest and easiest way to get to the centre of London was by the Underground. They left their cars at the fire station and twenty minutes later they were in the heart of the city.

The fire engine was parked on the edge of a small square, flanked by bars and shops, and there were still plenty of people on the street. As they walked towards it through the crowds, Callie could see that one side of the vehicle had been decorated to turn it into Santa's sleigh. There were carol singers and people were crowding around a warmly clad man in a Santa costume, who was helping children up into the driving seat.

Ben greeted the men already there and introduced Callie. Their names were lost in the music and chatter, but there were smiles and suddenly it didn't much matter who she was or why she was here. She was just one of the team.

A bundle of leaflets was pressed into Ben's hands and he set to work, wishing everyone a happy Christmas, in between singing along with the carols in a deep baritone. He placed leaflets in everyone's hands with a smiling exhortation to read them on the way home.

Callie picked up a leaflet that had fluttered to the ground. On one side were wishes for a safe and happy Christmas from the London Fire Brigade. On the other side was some basic fire safety advice that was easy to read and follow.

'So all this has an ulterior motive?' She saw Ben looking at her and she smiled.

'You could call it that. Although I reckon that having a house fire is one of the unhappier things that can happen to anyone, so it's really just a practical extension of us telling everyone to have a happy Christmas…'

He turned for a moment as a woman tapped his arm, responding to her question. 'Yes, that's the British Standards safety sign. Always make sure your tree lights carry it.'

'Okay. I'll check mine when I get home.'

'Great.' Ben gifted her with the kind of smile that would persuade the angels themselves to switch off their heavenly lights if they weren't up to safety standards and wished her a happy Christmas.

'Can I take some of those?' Callie pointed to the leaflets in his hand.

'Yes, of course. Don't you want to take some photographs?'

That was what she was there for but her camera was zipped under her coat and taking it out seemed like taking a step back from the circle of warmth and light around the fire engine. Realistically it was impossible to reduce the children's delight as they were lifted up into the driving seat to just one frame, so instead she took the opportunity to just feel the joy.

'Later maybe. I've got an interest in this, too.' As a paramedic, Callie didn't fight fires but she'd seen some of the of the injuries they caused.

He handed half his stack of leaflets to Callie. Ben didn't say a word but his grin spoke volumes. No more fighting each other. The season of peace and joy seemed to be working its magic.

CHAPTER FIVE

SUDDENLY IT FELT like Christmas. Callie was animated and smiling, approaching people on the edge of the crowd that had gathered around them and giving them leaflets. She seemed softer, warmer somehow. As if she'd dropped her defences and with them the hard edges that didn't quite suit her.

'Getting cold?' Even though she was never still, she couldn't disguise her red fingers. Gloves made it difficult to separate the leaflets and hand them out, and she'd taken hers off and stuffed them in her pocket.

'Yes, a little.' She smiled up at him, clearly not of a mind to let frozen fingers stop her.

'There are flasks with hot coffee...' He motioned up towards the cabin of the fire engine, which was now closed and dark. The families had all gone home now, and the crowd mainly consisted of revellers, wanting to squeeze the last moments from their pre-Christmas celebrations.

'So that's why everyone's been nipping up there every now and then? Why didn't you tell me sooner? I'd love some.'

'You have to give out at least a hundred leaflets before you get coffee.'

'Well, I've given out three handfuls. That must be a hundred so...' She gripped the front of his jacket in a mock threat. *'Give me my coffee, elf. Or else...'*

However much he wanted to warm up, standing his ground now seemed like a delicious moment that couldn't be missed. 'Or else what?'

'Or... I'll make you collect up all the old wrapping paper, peel the sticky tape off it and smooth it flat to use next year.' She grinned.

'In that case...' Submitting to the threat was another delicious moment that made the hairs on the back of Ben's neck stand to attention. 'This way, Santa.'

He led her over to the fire engine, opening the door for her, and Callie climbed up into the cockpit, sliding across to sit behind the wheel. Ben followed her, reaching for the three large flasks in the footwell. Two were already empty, but the third was heavy when he picked it up.

As he poured the coffee, he saw Callie's fingers touch the bottom of the steering wheel lightly, as if she was yearning to take hold of it and pretend to drive, the way kids did when you sat them in that seat. She was looking ahead of her, the bright Christmas lights reflecting in her face, softening her features. Or maybe it was just the look on her face.

'Thanks.' She wrapped her fingers around the cup, clearly wanting to warm them before she drank. Ben poured a second cup for himself and propped it on the dashboard. The only heat he wanted right now was the heat of her smile.

'You can try it out for size if you want.' He nodded towards the steering wheel. 'I won't tell anyone.'

The thought seemed tempting to her, but she shook her head. 'Bit late for that now.'

'It's never too late…' Ben let the thought roll in his head. It was an odd one, since he'd privately reckoned that it *was* too late for him.

And Callie seemed to think that too. She shook her head, turning to him with a smile. 'Did you sit in a fire engine when you were a kid?'

'All the time. My dad was a firefighter and he used to lift me up into the driving seat of the engines whenever my Mum took me to the fire station.'

'So you knew all along what you wanted to be when you grew up.'

'Yeah.' Ben wondered which side of her life had been a childhood dream. Photographer or paramedic. 'What did you want to be?'

'Safe…' The word had obviously escaped her lips before she had a chance to stop it, and Callie reddened a little.

'Safe is a good ambition.'

Her gaze met his, a trace of mockery in it. *Do you even know what safe is?* Ben realised that it was the last thing he'd have thought about wanting when he'd been a child. He always *had* been safe.

For a moment the questions he wanted to ask hung in the cold air. Then Callie shrugged, grinning. 'My dad died when I was six. He was a police officer and he was killed in the line of duty. That was when I found out that…anything can be taken away.'

'I'm sorry. I can't imagine how that must have felt.'

She shrugged. 'I'm not entirely sure how I feel about it either. How did *you* deal with the risks of your father's job?'

'I guess… I never had to think about them. He always came home.'

'And now? You must have thought about them when *you* joined the fire service.'

The question seemed important to her, and Ben thought carefully about his answer. 'There are some things that are important enough to take risks to achieve. Without that, a life can become meaningless. And we don't take risks for their own sake, you know that we're all about safety.'

Callie nodded silently. She didn't seem much convinced by his answer and Ben had the feeling he hadn't heard the whole story.

'But you never felt safe? As a child?'

'I did for a while. Mum remarried and I thought that we'd go back to being a family.' She shrugged. 'Her new husband ran up a pile of debts and then disappeared. We lost our house and pretty much everything we owned. After that it was horrible. Mum worked all the time and I was scared to be in our bedsit on my own. We got back on our feet but it was a struggle for her.'

Callie spoke almost dispassionately, as if she didn't care that she'd lost her father and then her home. In Ben's experience that meant she cared a great deal.

Nothing he could say felt enough. He reached for her hand, feeling a deep thankfulness when she didn't snatch it away.

'Here...' He guided her hand to the steering wheel, wrapping his over it. 'How does that feel?'

She gave a nervous laugh. 'That feels pretty good.'

'Try the other one.' He reached across, taking her coffee from the other hand, and Callie took hold of the steering wheel and gazed out ahead of her. Suddenly she laughed.

'Okay. You've made your point. I'm sitting on top of…how many horsepower?'

'About two hundred and fifty.'

'That much? And I'm looking over everyone's heads. It feels good.'

'Is powerful the word you're looking for?' Ben remembered the feeling of sitting behind the wheel when he was a child. Of being able to do anything, meet any challenge. That seemed to be the ultimate safety.

'That'll do.'

Suddenly he wanted very badly to kiss her. If he really could meet any challenge then perhaps he could meet this one? But Callie took her hands from the steering wheel and the spell was broken. She reached for her cup, wrapping her fingers around it again, and sipped the hot coffee.

Large snowflakes began to fall from the night sky, drifting down and melting as soon as they touched the pavement. Ben ignored them in favour of watching her face. It tipped upwards as the snowfall became heavier, a sudden taste of the magic of Christmas. Callie wasn't as unreachable as she tried to make out.

'There's always one, isn't there?' She quirked her lips down suddenly, and Ben could almost see the real world taking over from the imaginary. He followed her gaze, looking towards a couple of men in business suits and heavy over-coats, clearly involved in a drunken argument.

'Yep.' He wanted to tell her to disregard them. To come back with him to the world where it always snowed at Christmas, and where it was still possible to make up for all the things Callie hadn't had during her childhood. But one of the men suddenly took a swing at the other.

A space opened up around them as people moved out of the way. The argument seemed to become hotter and the carol singers faltered as the men's shouts reached their ears.

'So much for comfort and joy...' Ben muttered the words angrily, pulling the door of the fire engine open and getting out. A couple of the other firefighters were already on their way over to break up the fight.

But the brawlers were determined. One broke away from the firefighter who was crowding him back and threw a punch. The other slipped and fell, rolling on the icy pavement and curs-ing loudly. He tried to get unsteadily to his feet, and Ben could see blood running down the side of his face.

The men were separated quickly, with a min-imum of fuss, and Ben made for the one who'd been hurt. He was standing unsteadily now, half supported and half held back by two of the fire-fighters. Then Callie pushed past him, her head bare, the Santa hat protruding from her jacket pocket. She'd snapped back into paramedic mode.

'Let me see… Bring him over to the fire engine.'

Ben walked the man over to the truck, opening the door of the cabin and helping him inside. Callie climbed in on the other side and the man relaxed back into the seat, seeming to want to go to sleep.

'You're carrying a first-aid kit?'

'Yep.' It was about the only piece of working equipment that the fire engine still carried. He went to collect it, adding a flashlight, and handed both to Callie.

She carefully examined the man, trying to elicit a sensible answer to some simple questions, but he was too drunk to even tell her his name. Or he had a concussion. Ben knew that it was impossible for even Callie to tell.

The stench of sweat and alcohol filled the cabin but she seemed not to notice. She cleaned the blood from his face carefully, and it appeared that the cut on his forehead was deep but relatively minor.

Finally, she blew out a breath. 'He's probably just drunk, but he's hit his head and it looked as if he was unconscious for a few moments. He should go to the hospital. Is there anyone here with a car who can take him? I'd call an ambulance but on Christmas Eve…'

The ambulance service would be busy and there would be a wait. It was quicker to have someone take him.

'I think so. I'll ask…' Ben didn't want to leave her alone with the man. He was unpredictable, and at any moment he could lash out at her. He wound down the window and called to one of the men standing next to the fire engine.

'Hey…! Close it.' The cold air blowing into the cabin seemed to wake the man for a moment and he shivered.

'All right. We're going to take you to the hospital, so they can make sure you're okay.' Callie's voice betrayed a note of caring that the man almost certainly didn't deserve.

'No! Going home…' The man tried to climb over her to get out of the cabin, and Ben caught his arm before he elbowed Callie in the face.

'Stay put. And be quiet. You do what the lady tells you.' The threatening note that he injected into his tone was enough to subdue the man.

'My hero…' Callie rewarded him with a flashed smile and the murmured words, and he felt his chest swell in response.

Outside, the discussion amongst the other firefighters seemed to have come to some conclusion, and Ben saw one of them signal that he'd take the man when they were ready. Callie made one last examination and then opened the man's coat, looking for an inside pocket. Finding the man's phone, she switched it on and scrolled through the contacts list.

'This is your home number?'

The man reached out to snatch the phone from her, and Ben caught his arm before he could touch her. If he laid one finger on Callie, Ben might forget his training and be tempted to hurt him.

'Don't even think about it,' he growled at the man, opening the door to get him out of the cabin. Callie shot him a smile and dialled the number, speaking quietly into the phone.

The car drew up and he propelled the man into the back seat. Two of the other firefighters got in and, seeing that he was outnumbered, the man sat quietly, seeming to fall back into a drowse.

'Wait a minute. Callie's got his phone.' Ben looked round and saw that Callie had ended the call and was walking towards him.

'Shall I go with them? To the hospital?'

'No. The guys all have basic medical training, they can handle it. Jim will give them a lift home once they've taken him to the hospital.'

Callie hesitated, turning the corners of her mouth down. 'I spoke to his girlfriend and she said that he was meant to be home hours ago, and that we could leave him in a gutter for all she cared. She gave me his brother's number, though, and he says he'll pick him up from the hospital.'

'Fine. Just give the guys his number and they'll deal with it.'

Callie still looked unconvinced, but she handed over the phone to Jim, bending down to look into the back seat of the car to check on the man one last time. It seemed that she was repeating her offer to go with them and Jim was repeating what Ben had told her. The car started and Callie shrugged, turning her attention to the other man, who was sitting on a nearby bench, his elbows propped on his knees, staring at his feet.

'Are you okay?'

'No, not really. They're taking Carl to hospital?'

'It's just a precaution. We don't think he's hurt, but he's drunk and he's hit his head. He needs to be checked over.'

'My sister's going to kill me. Carl's girlfriend...'

Ben saw Callie's lips press together momentarily. 'I dare say that everything will work out.' She'd clearly decided not to share what Carl's girlfriend had said to her on the phone.

'Yeah, right. She'll start talking to my wife...' The man shook his head. 'She wanted me to be home before the kids went to bed. I said we were just going out for a quick drink...'

'We'll get a taxi for you.' Ben decided it was time to step in. 'You're sure you feel okay?'

'Dead man walking, mate. You know how it is.' The man grinned at Ben, as if he was in league with him.

He could almost feel Callie's anger. She took a step forward and he reached out automatically, touching her arm. She heeded the silent warning and turned suddenly, walking away.

She looked so alone suddenly, standing with the firefighters, who were still giving out leaflets to the last of the passers-by. It was getting late, and there were few enough of them now, and Callie seemed silent and preoccupied. Common sense told him that he should leave her alone for a moment and she'd cool down, but Ben couldn't do it.

'Forget it.'

She was staring at her feet now, shivering with cold. 'I just... It's Christmas, for crying out loud. Couldn't they have just taken one night off and gone home? Been where they ought to be?'

'I know. But you can't let it get to you. No one can change what happened to you when you were a kid, but you can take *this* Christmas back. Wrestle it to the ground if you have to, beat it into submission and show it who's boss.' He reached for the Santa hat, pulling it out of her pocket and putting it firmly back onto her head, pulling it down over her ears.

She looked up at him suddenly. For a moment he thought he saw the magic again, reflected in her troubled eyes, but it was probably only the lights strung along the side of the fire engine. Suddenly she smiled, adjusting the hat to a jauntier angle on her head.

'All right. Are there any leaflets left?'

'A few…' Ben picked up the last of them and split the pile into two, giving her half. 'You want to see who can get rid of theirs first?'

She rose to the challenge. Of course she did, she didn't know what else to do with a challenge other than meet it headlong. But when Ben turned to watch her, she seemed suddenly so very alone in a crowd where everyone seemed to have someone.

CHAPTER SIX

CHRISTMAS DAY DAWNED bright and clear. Callie was up early and on the road almost before she was properly awake. The fire station was thrumming with noise and light when she arrived, but the noise was that of sirens, and the lights flashed blue in the morning mist.

It wasn't just another working day, though. Everyone smiled and wished each other a happy Christmas, and between calls there were mince pies and a roast dinner, eaten in haste before the next call came in. But peace and joy brought oven fires, wrapping-paper fires and even a patio fire, where one brave soul had thought it a good idea to finish the turkey off on the barbeque.

Ben had been relaxed and jocular—there was nothing that Blue Watch couldn't deal with easily and the arrival of a fire engine brought extra interest, people coming from their houses with Christmas fare and good wishes for the firefighters. A young boy was cut from where he'd got lodged in the park railings, with the minimum of fuss, and seemed none the worse for the experience.

Callie photographed it all, working side by side with the crew. It seemed that Christmas Day was going to end with no serious damage to life and limb, but just as darkness was beginning to fall, the call came.

There was no room for her in the disciplined scramble. Ben took a moment to call an address to her and then Callie was left to her own devices. She waited until the fire engine was out of the garage, the sirens retreating into the distance, and then got into her car.

When she arrived, Blue Watch was already in action, along with three other teams that were in attendance. Fire was spurting from the windows on one side of a large, two-storey block of flats. Callie didn't need to be told to stay back out of the way. She knew that her presence would only hamper the men and women who were struggling to get the fire under control. She could see the firefighters of Blue Watch donning breathing equipment, ready to go inside.

She raised her camera and then lowered it. This wasn't a scene for calendar shots. Maybe afterwards, once it was clear that there had been no casualties.

All the same, she watched. Counting the firefighters of Blue Watch in and hearing her heart beat out the seconds and minutes before she could count them back out again. Ben had been the first in and she hadn't seen him come out yet.

Then he appeared in the doorway, a small bundle wrapped in his arms, protected from the smoke that curled around him. Behind him came a woman, supported by two firefighters.

The ambulance crew ran forward and Ben delivered the bundle to them. The woman was being helped to the waiting ambulance, reaching towards the child that Ben had brought out of the building. Tears blurred Callie's vision and she felt a lump rise at the back of her throat.

He tore the mask from his face and bent over in a movement of sudden weariness. Callie knew that the heavy equipment and the difficult conditions inside the building could exhaust even the fittest man quickly. But Ben took only a moment to catch his breath, walking over to the tender and gulping down water from a bottle. Then he turned, motioning to another two of the firefighters, including Eve. He was going back in again.

Callie turned away. She couldn't watch this. But she couldn't not watch either. The thought that little Isaac might not see his mother tonight… Or that she might not see Ben again.

She had to get a grip. Ben was doing what he had to and he was part of a team. No one would be hurt and no one would be left behind. Callie had attended plenty of scenes like this and she'd done her job, tending to those who'd been hurt. It was not having any job to do that was killing her.

Looking around, she saw a small family group sitting huddled together on a bench. Holding each other tight as they watched silently. No one seemed to be taking much notice of them and Callie walked over.

'Hello. Have you been seen by anyone? I'm a paramedic.'

The man looked up at her and Callie saw tears in his eyes. 'Yes. Thanks. We got out as soon as we heard the alarms go off.'

'You must be cold.' The woman had a baby in her arms, which she was holding inside her coat. There was a little girl of about six, who was swathed in a coat that was obviously her father's and the man wore just a sweater.

He looked up at her as if the idea of warmth or cold didn't really register. Just shock, and concern for his family.

'Do you have somewhere to go?' Callie sat down on the end of the bench. If she could be of no help to the fire and ambulance crews, maybe she could do something here.

'Yeah. My wife's brother…'

'He's coming to collect us.' The woman spoke quietly. 'He's driving down from Bedford.'

'It'll be a little while before he arrives, then. My car's over there. Why don't you come with me and get warm?'

The whole family had piled into the back seat, seeming unable to let go of each other. Callie had got behind the wheel and started the engine so she could put the heaters on full for a while, and as the windows started to mist up, the woman told her that her name was Claire and her husband was Mike. Then the little girl spoke up.

'What's your name?'

'I'm Callie. What's yours?'

'Anna.' Now that she'd emerged from the wrappings of her father's coat, Callie could see blonde hair tied up in a ponytail with a red and green ribbon, and a red pinafore dress over a green sweater. Anna was looking around her, adapting to her new situation with the kind of resilience that only a child could muster.

'Are you taking pictures?' Anna's eye lit on the camera in Callie's lap.

'Not at the moment. But I've been at the fire station today, taking photographs.'

Anna frowned, and her mother reached out to her, smoothing a stray lock of hair from her face. 'There's always someone at the fire station, even on Christmas Day, sweetie. When they hear that there's a fire, they come quickly and put it out.'

'But…' Anna rubbed the condensation from the window with her hand, staring outside. 'It's not out yet.'

'Sometimes it takes a little while. But they won't leave until the fire's out.' Callie tried to sound reassuring.

'I left my presents behind…in my room.' Tears began to form in Anna's eyes. Her parents had clearly tried to shield her from the gravity of the situation, and she didn't know how much she'd lost yet, but she was beginning to work it out for herself.

Mike held his daughter tight. 'Everything's going to be all right, button. We're going to Uncle Joe's and we'll stay there for a little while. All that matters is that we're safe and we're together, and when we come back again I'll make sure everything's as good as new.'

'You…promise?'

'Yes, darling. I promise.'

Callie swallowed down the lump that formed in her throat. Opening the glove compartment, she found the bar of chocolate that was usually stowed away in there. It was all she had to comfort the child.

'Hey, Anna. Would you like to share this with your mum and dad?' She tore the wrapper open and broke the chocolate into squares.

Anna took the chocolate, holding a square up

to her mother's lips. Claire smiled and opened her mouth. The little girl solemnly fed her father a square and then picked the biggest one for herself.

As the flames subsided, it became possible for the firefighters to rest a little longer than just the time it took them to get back on their feet. Ben had waited until each of his crew had taken their turn to have a ten-minute break, and then his chance came. He stood alone, scanning the people who stood beyond the police line.

She wasn't there. Somehow Callie had opened up a hole in his life that hadn't existed before. Something missing, which he'd never thought about until now.

He should turn away and find something else to do. Taking his break, sitting down and getting his breath would be a good idea because he suddenly felt very weary. But when he looked again, he saw Callie's car parked some way up the street, shadows on the rear window indicating that it wasn't empty. Before he knew what he was doing, Ben had started to walk towards it, drawn by the inescapable urge to just see her.

As he passed through the police cordon he removed his helmet and gloves, finding that he was wiping his face with one hand. He hadn't bothered before, and there was no way he could wipe away the grime and soot, but still he ran his fingers through his hair to flatten it a bit, feeling it rough and caked with sweat and dirt.

As he approached, the car door opened and she got out, smiling breathlessly in a good imitation of the way that Ben himself felt.

'You're...okay?'

Warmth swelled in his heart. He was okay now.

'Yes.'

She took a step forward as if to hug him and Ben stepped back. The filth on his jacket would spoil everything. He wanted her just as she was now, untouched by the ravages of fire, a bright, gleaming reminder that life would go on. Now he understood why the parents in his crew went home and just stared at their sleeping kids.

He pointed to the car, searching for something to say that didn't betray his joy at seeing her. 'They escaped from the fire? Are they all okay?'

'Yes, they got out as soon as they heard the alarm. Their flat's on the ground floor...' She pointed to the left-hand side of the building in an obvious question. How bad was it? Ben could see a small head bobbing between the two adults who sat in the back seat and felt his heart bang in his chest.

'The fire damage isn't as bad on that side. But

everywhere… It's all going to be waterlogged, Callie. Do they have somewhere to go?'

'Yes, they have family coming to collect them from Bedford. They'll be here soon.' Callie's look of disappointment couldn't have been more acute if it had been her own home.

There was nothing he could say. All Ben could do was wonder whether Callie was reliving the time when she'd lost her home as a child. The back door of the car opened and a man got out, holding a little girl in his arms. Instantly, the loss and the heartbreak on Callie's face was replaced by a smile.

'I want to thank you.' The man held out his hand to Ben and he shook it, muttering his regrets that they hadn't been able to save their home.

'That doesn't matter. My wife and my kids are safe. Everyone else got out?'

Ben nodded an assent. Then the little girl called his name.

How did she know? Perhaps Callie had seen him walking over and had told the family. Then Callie grinned. 'I've been showing Anna some of the pictures I took back at the fire station. I'm not sure *I* would have recognised you with all that grime on your face.'

Suddenly he felt self-conscious, as if he'd turned up for a date with a piece of broccoli caught in his teeth. Ben shook off the feeling. He'd just been fighting a fire, for goodness' sake, and Callie was no stranger to people not looking their best in an emergency situation.

'Daddy, I want to take a picture...'

The man laughed. It was an incongruous sound amongst the noise of destruction, but when he looked at his daughter the stress lines on his face disappeared for a moment. 'I'm sure that Ben has better things to do, sweetie...'

'That's okay. Everything's under control and I've got a short break.' Ben glanced behind him to check again that he wasn't needed for a few minutes.

'Why don't I take the picture? You can be in it.' Callie addressed the child and she nodded.

Her camera was on a lanyard around her neck, but she turned back briefly to the car, fetching something from the front seat. It was a small compact camera, and Ben wondered why she would choose that one. Anna was lowered from her father's arms and Callie took the warm coat, which was far too big for her, from her shoulders to reveal a red and green Christmas outfit.

'Go and stand next to Ben, Anna. Try not to touch him, you'll get yourself all dirty.'

Ben sank to his knees next to the child. She was fresh and clean and, above all, safe. *This.*

This was why he'd chosen his job and why he continued to do it.

'This is what we do at the fire station.' He folded his arms, smiling into the camera. 'Comrades…'

Anna glanced at Callie and she grinned. 'Comrades means friends. Everyone stands in a straight line, folding their arms.' She clearly understood Ben's reticence to leave a smudge on the child's hand by holding it.

Anna got the idea. Standing to attention, as straight as she could, she folded her arms. Through a daze of fatigue Ben heard Callie laugh, and new strength began to surge through him.

She seemed to be taking her time, which was unusual for Callie, who saw a shot and took it almost as naturally as breathing. When she was done, and Anna ran back into her father's arms, he realised why. She'd used both cameras.

Anna's father called out a thank-you, wrapping the coat around his daughter again. Callie motioned them back into the car, giving them the compact camera in response to Anna's demands to see her pictures. He and Callie were alone again for a precious few moments.

'Where did she get the camera from?' Ben reckoned he knew. It seemed unlikely that the family, who hadn't stopped to pick up their child's own coat, would have chosen a camera as the one thing to save from their home.

Callie shrugged it off. 'I keep a back-up camera in the boot.'

'Looks brand new to me.' The camera still had some of the manufacturer's stickers on it. Ben shot her a glance, which said she couldn't get away with this act of kindness without someone noticing, and she reddened a little.

'So it's new. My old one was on its last legs, so I bought a new one and happened to have it in the boot of my car. Knock it off, Ben. It's Christmas Day…' Callie's steel resurfaced, all the more captivating because he knew that it concealed a heart of gold, which knew what it was like to be a child with no presents on Christmas Day.

He lost the chance to tell her that she'd made a generous gesture. A shout behind him turned her attention to a man running up the road towards them and Anna's father got out of the car, waving in response.

'That must be their lift…'

And she would want to say goodbye to Anna. Maybe hug her. The thought didn't seem so outrageous as it would have a few days ago, now he'd seen the evidence of Callie's softer side. 'I've got to get on. You're going straight home from here?'

The thought that he wouldn't get to touch her

tore at his heart. Maybe he wouldn't need to so badly after he'd had a shower and changed his clothes, but now it was all that Ben could think about.

'No, I thought I'd see them off and then go back to the fire station…' She shot him an agonised look, which effortlessly penetrated the layers of protective clothing that shielded his heart. Maybe Callie wanted to be close to him as much as he wanted to be close to her. The idea fanned the flames that flickered in his chest.

'I'll see you there, then.' With an effort, he turned his attention to Anna, who was sitting in the back seat of the car, cuddled up close to her mother. The little girl seemed tearful now, and perhaps the reality of leaving her home behind, which Callie had somehow managed to hold back, was dawning on her.

Anna managed a smile and a wave, and her father shook his hand again. Then Ben turned, not daring to take another look at Callie before he walked back to his crew.

CHAPTER SEVEN

IT WAS LONG past the time when his shift had ended, but Ben seemed in no hurry. He'd made time to exchange a few words with every member of his crew, trading jokes and casual goodbyes, which had somewhat covered the fact that he was clearly checking on everyone.

Callie had reckoned that seeing him showered and dressed in clean clothes might dispel the image of him walking towards her car, clearly exhausted and caked in grime. She hadn't been in any danger but he'd seemed like a hero, coming to carry her away and save her.

But it didn't. He seemed just as handsome, just as much the kind of man who might buck the trend and show her that it was possible to rely on someone and not get hurt. Callie dismissed the thought, reminding herself that she'd needed saving a long time ago. Her life was on track now and she was just fine on her own. If seeing Ben smile at Anna had awakened the thought that Christmas could bring unexpected presents, then this one had arrived far too late to change anything.

'Did you take any photographs?' She was sitting in the ready room, fiddling with her camera, trying to pretend that she wasn't waiting her turn for Ben to speak to her. She wasn't a part of his crew so maybe he didn't reckon that was necessary.

'A big fire like that isn't really the kind of thing to put on a calendar. People get hurt…' She felt herself redden.

'Yeah. You came anyway.'

'Well, it turned out that I could make myself useful.'

He grinned, as if this was exactly the thing he'd wanted her to say. 'That little girl's going to remember the person who gave her a camera when she had nothing else on Christmas Day. Maybe it'll make another little girl feel a bit better, too.'

The other little girl being Callie. The fearful child who knew that life was quite capable of taking everything she had, if she wasn't careful.

'Enough, Ben. I'm not in the mood for deep and meaningful at the moment.' Callie picked up her camera. 'Can I have one last shot? You by the Christmas tree?'

'Now I'm a little cleaner?' He got the point

immediately. It was all about the contrasts, the rigour of his work and the winding-down process afterwards. He went and stood by the tree in the corner of the room, folding his arms.

Callie raised the camera, took a couple of shots in the hope that might make him relax a bit, and then lowered it. 'That's not quite right. Perhaps you could try looking a bit more awkward?'

Ben laughed uneasily. Some people smiled when they looked into a lens and some people froze. He was a freezer. The only really good posed shot she'd been able to get of him had been the one she'd taken with Anna, when Ben had been too exhausted to think about feeling self-conscious.

He uncrossed his arms, shifted from one foot to the other and then crossed his arms again. 'What do you want me to do with my hands?'

There was an answer to that but Callie wasn't going to give it. 'Try… No, not like that. You look like my sixth form biology teacher.'

He shook his head. 'I have *no* idea what that means…' For a moment Callie thought that she was going to get the relaxed shot that she was looking for, and then he stiffened up again. If all his smiles were that cardboard, she'd have no problem resisting them.

She took another couple of pictures and then

gave up. She'd have to sneak up on him later. 'Okay, that's good. Thanks.'

Ben relaxed and walked back towards her. *That* was the shot she wanted but she'd already put her camera down and it was too late.

'Are you ready to go? I'll walk you to your car.' He picked up his jacket from the back of the chair. Callie nodded, picking her coat up and following him out of the building.

The car park was deserted. Just him and her, and a biting wind. Ben stopped next to Callie's car, as if that was the most natural thing in the world.

'I'm glad you're safe.' She was closer to him now, the sleeve of her coat almost touching his.

'Me too. It's…' He shrugged. 'We balance the risks and eliminate them…'

'Yes, I know. I'm still glad you're safe.' Leaving now without touching him might just trigger another emergency situation. One where she'd have to be hauled clear and revived. Because Callie felt that she wouldn't be able to breathe without Ben.

He didn't want her to make a fuss. He did this kind of thing all the time and so did the other firefighters.

Who are you trying to kid, Ben? He wanted Callie to make as much fuss as possible. He wanted to comfort her and then have her make a fuss all over again.

She was so close and yet not close enough. His hand drifted to hers, his fingers brushing the back of her hand. And then suddenly she flung her arms around his shoulders.

'This doesn't mean...' She buried her face in his shoulder, holding him tight.

'Anything...' Ben used the same excuse as she did to wind his arms around her waist. The cool-down after an emergency, when everything seemed so much simpler. The adrenaline still coursing in his veins and the feeling that everyday concerns didn't matter so much.

But it *did* mean something. He brushed his lips across her forehead, knowing that was never going to be enough, and felt her body move against his as she stretched up.

When he kissed her lips, it felt like all the Christmases he'd ever had rolled up in one big, beautiful parcel. It felt like a summer breeze, an autumn chill and the raging heat of an open fire, crackling and spitting as the flames blew hot and hard. Callie responded to him with just the right measure of softness and passion.

And then the fire subsided. They'd reminded themselves what it was like to be alive and safe this Christmas, and now it was time to let her go. But Ben couldn't.

'When you get home…' he linked his hands loosely behind her back '…and you switch on the lights on your Christmas tree…'

She shook her head. 'No Christmas tree this year.'

'What?' The image of Callie sitting next to her Christmas tree, drinking a toast to him at the same moment that he drank one to her, dissolved. It had been his last chance of walking away from her.

'What kind of person are you?'

She smiled up at him. 'One who's working over Christmas?'

No. Callie was the kind of person who knew exactly what a bleak Christmas was like. The kind of person who could prove to herself that she was strong enough for it not to matter by not caring about Christmas now. He wouldn't allow it.

'I have a tree. With lights. And I have sherry, and turkey sandwiches, and Christmas cake…'

'No! What are you, the Christmas mafia?'

He bent, whispering in her ear, 'I have red and green paper napkins. And board games. They're quite old, though, they're the ones I used to play when I was a kid.'

She laughed, nudging at his shoulder with her hand. 'Enough! I could drop in for an hour, I suppose. Since we're not back on shift again until Boxing Day evening.'

'My thoughts exactly.' The watch rota was two days and then two nights, separated by a twenty-four-hour break. Ben usually stayed up as late as he could after the second day, sleeping in, so he'd be fresh for his first night's work.

He took her car keys from her hand, unlocking it, and opened the driver's door. 'You'll follow me?'

'Yes, I'll follow you.'

Ben had given her the address and watched her punch it into the satnav, but even so Callie had stayed behind him, following him into the east end of London. Two cars, almost alone on the dark streets, winding through the hodgepodge of old buildings, most of which had been refurbished and given a new lease of life, making the area a vibrant and exciting place to live. He drew up outside a pair of iron gates, and they swung open, allowing them into a small parking area.

'What is this place?' Callie looked around at the massive building, which seemed to once have housed something industrial.

'It's an old warehouse.' Ben punched a combination into a keypad and swung the heavy entrance doors open, leading the way through a small lobby. A staircase ran around a large, commercial-sized lift and he pulled back the old-fashioned gates.

'It's got a lot of character.' Callie looked around her as she stepped into the lift. The lobby was bright and clean, paint having been applied directly onto the exposed brickwork to preserve the industrial feel.

'That's the nice way of putting it. When we bought this place we didn't have the funds to do more than just clean up and get everything working properly.'

'You did this?'

'A group of us. A friend of mine is an architect, and the company that owned this place was one of his clients. They were going to convert it into luxury apartments, but they only got as far as stripping it out and adding the internal walls to form separate living spaces before they ran out of money. They were selling the building at a bargain price, so my friend got a group together and we bought it.'

They stood on opposite sides of the lift as it ascended slowly. The drive, and this talk about home improvements hadn't diminished Callie's desire to touch him again, but she was handling it. Callie cleared her throat.

'How many apartments here?' She tried to make the question sound as if the information was vital to her.

Ben's smile made her shiver. He knew that this was all just a delicious game, that they'd play for an hour and then she'd go. And he seemed okay with that.

'Twelve. They were just shells when we bought the place, and each of us had a lot of work to do. It helped a lot having an architect on the team, because he knew how to undertake a big building project, what we could do ourselves and what we needed a contractor and a project manager for.'

The lift drifted to a halt on the third floor, and Ben drew back the gates, turning right to one of the two doors at either side of the hallway.

Callie was expecting something unusual, but when he opened the door to his apartment, ushering her inside, she was still surprised. A large, open space, the vaulted ceiling supported by round pillars and heavy metal beams. At the far end, a mezzanine had what seemed to be a sleeping area above it and a kitchen and dining area below. And in here it was most definitely Christmas.

Ben flipped a switch and the tree standing by the tall windows lit up. Fairy lights from top to bottom glimmered against gold baubles and frosted-glass icicles. Swags of greenery, mixed with tinsel and fairy lights ran along the length of the metal railings that edged the mezzanine. He walked over to a large brick fireplace surrounded by easy chairs and a sofa and turned the gas fire on, the leaping flames making the ornaments on the tree sparkle.

'This is… It's like something out of a magazine. I couldn't do it.'

Ben laughed, stowing her coat away in one of the built-in cupboards by the door and making for the kitchen. 'You're the photographer. I think you could do a lot better.'

Maybe with the small things. But the grand plan was beyond anything that Callie could conceive of doing. 'I wouldn't have the courage to put everything into a project like this. I'd think about it and then decide to play it safe and stick with what I had.'

Ben lost interest in the contents of the fridge, looking round suddenly. 'That's a bit of a recurring theme for you, isn't it? Playing things safe. I'd guess it's something you've learned and it doesn't come naturally to you.'

He was breaking the rules. This game of dropping round on Christmas night for sandwiches and board games shouldn't include anything more personal than whether she wanted cranberry sauce with her turkey. She walked over to the breakfast bar and sat down on one of the high stools that faced into the kitchen.

'Okay, I'll play. Why don't you think it comes naturally to me?'

'Because... Most people with a talent for something would stay in the nine-to-five and think, *If only.* You've gone out and made a success of your photography, and that takes a bit of self-belief and a lot of guts.'

Callie hadn't thought of it that way. 'It's nice of you to say that. But I never really thought of my photography as a decision.'

'Don't you think that everything's a decision? Even if we don't really think about it?' Ben took a cold turkey breast from the fridge and started to cut slices from it.

'It didn't look as if you were stopping to make any decisions today when you went into that building.' She'd resolved not to ask Ben about that but she couldn't help herself.

He laid the knife down. 'I made that decision a long time ago, when I joined the fire service. I don't want to be the person who stands by and watches, not able to do anything to change things.'

'Despite the risk?'

'I take a calculated risk, which is always minimised by training and preparedness. You're a paramedic. How many of your patients walked out of their homes, assuming they were safe without even thinking about it, and then something happened to them?'

He had a point. 'Most of them.' Callie snagged

a piece of turkey from the pile. She didn't usually talk about any of this. Correction. She *never* talked about any of this. But, then, she didn't do Christmas either, and here she was, eating cold turkey and admiring a tree.

'So what made you make the decision to put up a tree, cook a turkey breast for sandwiches, and then spend Christmas alone?'

'I was working. In case you hadn't noticed.'

'That's no excuse. And you're not working now.'

'I'm not on my own either. You're here.' Callie raised her eyebrows and he shrugged. 'I had a bad break-up just after Christmas last year. I decided to go this one alone.'

So there it was. Two people who wanted to be alone had ended up together. This Christmas just wasn't going to give up.

Ben finished making the sandwiches and took the mince pies from the oven, sliding them onto a plate. Everything went onto a tray, along with forks and side plates, and he carried it over to the easy chairs, which were grouped around a coffee table in front of the hearth.

'I have juice and ginger beer...' He walked back to the kitchen, taking two glasses from the cupboard and flipping the door closed. Callie remembered that she was intending to drive tonight.

'Ginger beer's fine. Don't let me stop you if you want a drink, though.'

He thought for a moment, obviously tempted, and then shook his head. 'No. I think I'll join you.'

CHAPTER EIGHT

CALLIE HAD WOLFED down her sandwiches, slowing a little for the mince pies, and now she was relaxed, slipping off her boots and tucking her feet up under her. Ben reached for the bottle of ginger beer and refilled her glass.

'Thanks. Cheers.' She stretched across the table, clinking her glass against his, and took a sip. 'So, were you serious about the board games?'

'Deadly serious.' Ben gestured towards the cabinet that held games he'd played practically every Christmas since he'd been a child. 'You get to choose which one, and I get to beat you at it.'

'You wish.' She got to her feet, making a thorough inspection of the contents of the cabinet. 'Snakes and Ladders. I haven't played that in years…'

'Good choice. I always win at Snakes and Ladders.' Ben grinned at her, and she carried the box over, opening it and laying out the board and pieces on the table.

'I always win too. So watch out.' She dropped the dice into the plastic cup and pushed it towards him. Delicious, competitive tension suddenly zinged in the air between them, like the promise of something forbidden.

His first throw took him to an empty square and Callie's took her to a short ladder. Ben picked up the dice, blowing on his fingers, and threw a six, which took him to the foot of a long ladder stretching halfway up the board.

'It's like that, is it?' Her gaze was on his face as she threw the dice again, and when she looked down at the board she wailed in frustration. 'No! A snake!'

'Admit it now. You're going to lose…'

She made a face at him, sliding her piece down the snake's body before taking a sip of her drink and taking her sweater off.

Ben looked back into her face and saw a smile that was beyond mischief.

If she was trying to make him so befuddled that he couldn't even count the squares, she was making a good job of it. Ben shook the dice and moved his piece. Two more moves each, which proved beyond any doubt that when snakes became suddenly interesting, ladders and empty squares were all you got.

'Ha!' Callie exclaimed in triumph as his next move took him right into the mouth of a long red and green snake, which wound its way almost to the bottom of the board.

'It *is* getting warm in here.' He pulled his sweater over his head. One look at Callie told him that he hadn't needed to voice the disclaimer. They both knew exactly where this was headed.

She landed on a snake. Her hand drifted to the buttons of her shirt, and Ben felt a bead of sweat trickle down his spine before he realised that no gentleman would allow her to do this. 'You could... A sock would be just fine, you know.'

'Where's the fun in that?'

Right now a mere inch of bare flesh, even if it was just an ankle, was likely to drive him crazy. Buttons would be a point of no return.

'I didn't... This isn't why I asked you here...'

'It's not why I came.' She turned the corners of her mouth down. 'Should I go?'

'No...' If she went now, she'd tear away the greater part of him. 'I really want you to stay.'

'A little Christmas madness?' She regarded him with a clear-eyed gaze. Such beautiful eyes, which seemed to see right through him.

'Just because it's not for keeps, it doesn't make it madness.' When she'd kissed him, it had been sheer magic.

Maybe she felt the same as he did, that *not for keeps* gave them both the freedom to do whatever they wanted tonight. Callie unbuttoned her shirt slowly, seeming to know that he wanted to watch every movement she made.

Even though she was wearing a sleeveless vest underneath, her bare arms and the curve of her breasts beneath the thin cotton were almost more than he could bear. It was an effort to tear his gaze from her, but somehow he managed to throw the dice and count the squares, knowing that this game was far too good not to be pushed to the point where neither of them could stand it any more.

They played in silence, smiling at each other across the board. A ladder each, and then Callie landed on another snake.

'Just my luck!' She puffed out a breath, sliding her piece back down the board.

'Why don't you let me take this one for you…?' Ben unbuttoned his shirt, feeling suddenly self-conscious. He wanted more than anything for her to like what she saw.

She did. He could see it in her face. The muscles across his shoulders tightened as the temperature climbed steadily higher.

He worked out. Of course he did, he had to be fit for his job. But right now it seemed as if someone were unwrapping the best Christmas present she could think of right in front of her eyes.

Callie wanted to jump across the table and tear at his clothes.

But she didn't. Their initial hesitancy had set the pace. Slow and so deliciously tantalising.

She watched as he cupped the dice in his hands, blowing on them for luck, while he grinned wickedly. Ben was unafraid of his own body, not bothering to suck his stomach in or square his shoulders. He didn't need to, he was perfect, and his lack of self-consciousness just made him even more so.

He landed on a ladder. Callie grinned.

'Winning move...' His smile was deliciously wicked. 'What have you got to divert my attention from that?'

'A sock?' She teased him.

'I'll take a sock. As long as I can be the one to take it off...'

'Yes...'

Suddenly he was all movement, pushing the board to one side and stepping across the table. Then he fell to his knees in front of her and Callie shivered. It was all she could do not to reach out and touch him.

Ben propped her foot on his leg, slowly pulling her sock off. And then the other one...

'Hey! Are you cheating?'

'Yep. Are you arguing?'

'No.'

Callie slid to the edge of the chair, winding her legs around his back and pulling him close. His skin was smooth and warm, brute strength rippling beneath its surface. In one bold, swift movement he pulled her vest over her head, kissing her as if she was the one thing in the world that he truly possessed.

Right now she was. When his movements slowed, tender now, she began to tremble. His hand lingered for a moment over the catch at the back of her bra in an implied question, and Callie reached behind her, undoing it for him. She felt his lips curve into a smile against hers as he gently pulled the straps from her shoulders.

'Your skin… *So* soft…' His fingers were exploring her back, her breasts crushed against his chest. Callie moved against him, desperate for a little friction, groaning in frustrated impatience when it wasn't enough.

'Look sharp…' She whispered the words that Ben called when he wanted to hurry the crew along, and he chuckled.

'Is this an emergency?'

'Yeah. I'm calling a Code Red…' she gasped into his ear, clinging to his shoulders.

He didn't let her down. Getting to his feet, he lifted her up in his arms, striding to the curved staircase. The mezzanine was dark, but in the fairy lights strung along the railings Callie could see a bed. That was all they needed.

He laid her down, pushing her hands away when she reached for the button on the waistband of his jeans. He was going to let her watch.

As he stripped off the rest of his clothes, the power in his body seemed to seep through her veins. She *had* to have him inside her. Callie wriggled on the bed, pulling at the zip of her trousers, but she was too slow. Ben had it, and was slowly drawing them down over her hips, kissing her burning skin as he went.

'One minute…' When she was finally naked, he backed away suddenly, grinning.

'What? Where are you going?'

He disappeared through a door leading to a walled-in space at the side of the open balcony. Bathroom? Callie heard the sound of glass crashing and breaking on a tiled surface, but Ben was clearly in too much of a hurry to stop and clear it up, because he appeared in the doorway moments later.

'You didn't forget these, did you?' He was holding a packet of condoms in his hand.

'You remembered for me…' Callie felt suddenly foolish. She never relied on a partner to take care of things like this.

'Only just.' He slung the condoms onto the bed, crawling towards her and covering her body with his. 'All I can think about is what I want to do with you.'

'And what I'll do with you?' She liked it that he was just as lost in this as she was.

'Yeah. Particularly that…' He guided her hand between her legs. Waiting for the clues she gave about exactly where and how she wanted to be touched, and when he had them his fingers took over from hers. *So* much better.

'Where else…?' He whispered the words against her ear, chuckling when Callie moved her hand to her breast. 'Of course…'

No more words now, because his tongue and lips were busy with an altogether more pleasurable exercise. Ben took her gasps as a challenge, pinning her down and turning them into moans. When he slipped one finger inside her, everything suddenly focussed on that one spot.

She fought the overwhelming urge to be taken, now, because there was something she wanted to do much more. Somewhere she found the strength to push him off her, over onto his back.

Her gaze held his as she planted kisses on his chest, moving downwards. His hands moved to her shoulders, his fingers trembling lightly on her skin. Callie watched the anticipation build in his face, and then his head snapped back suddenly, his body arching.

'Do that again…' It was practically a command.

'Do *what* again?' This time she used her tongue to caress him instead of her fingers. His groan told Callie that he was heading right to the place she wanted him. Joining her, on the edge of madness.

They pushed each other further. With each caress she wanted him more, until finally there was no resisting it. Ben held her down on the bed, fumbling with the condom with one hand. And then he was inside her, moving with all the urgency of a man with only one thought in his head.

She could feel herself beginning to come, and there was nothing she could do to stop it. Nothing she wanted to do. Pinned down by his weight, she could only respond to his driving rhythm. Callie choked out his name, digging her fingernails into his back, and then let go. She let go of everything she'd ever cared about, everything she'd ever wanted, turning herself over completely to Ben.

CHAPTER NINE

SHE WAS SO SWEET. So incredibly sexy. And physically they were a perfect match. She liked hot and hard, crazy desire that had blown Ben's mind to smithereens.

She liked lazy, tender lovemaking as much as he did, too. Feeling himself harden again inside her, and feeling her soften as he whispered in her ear. He told her she was beautiful and felt her cheek flush with pleasure against his. Callie's smile filled him with the kind of warmth that Ben knew he could only take for a little while. But that little while was now.

They made love until they were exhausted and then slept. Got out of bed to eat something and then made love again, and slept until the Boxing Day sun was low on the horizon.

'Do you know the way back to the fire station?' He swallowed down the hope that they might take just his car, leaving hers here so she'd have to return with him to pick it up.

She nodded. 'I'll find it. Maximum deniability, right?'

She had a point. Ben took the toast from the toaster and put two pieces on a plate, pushing it across the kitchen counter towards her. She nodded a thank-you and set about layering it with butter and apricot conserve.

'I like your hair…like that.' After they'd showered, her hair had dried in curls. It made her look soft and sexy, and Ben ventured the compliment even though he guessed that straight hair went a little better with the image that she wanted to project to the world.

'Do you?' She rubbed her hand across her head. 'I always think it makes me look a bit ditzy.'

Ben snorted in laughing disbelief. 'No. A little softer but definitely not ditzy.'

She grinned. 'Maybe I'll leave it for today, then. Where are my clothes?' She was wearing his towelling robe, which Ben privately thought looked a great deal better on Callie than it did on him.

'I put them in the washer-dryer while you were asleep. They'll be dry now.'

'You are a dream. You buy apricot conserve, you have a full fridge and you do my washing. Any chance I might kidnap you?'

Something tugged hard in Ben's chest. The

voice of reason had been strangely silent up till now, but it was back in full force, reminding him that he couldn't take even the slightest suggestion that he was ready for a full-time relationship.

'Not really…' He shook his head, and heard her laugh as he turned away from her, pretending that the coffee machine needed his immediate attention.

'I know. Only joking. I'm not looking to keep you for much longer.'

If he were in any other place in his life, the sudden reappearance of the other side to Callie's nature, the hard shell that kept everyone at arm's length, would have been disappointing. The fact that it was strangely comforting reminded Ben that he was in no position to deal with anything other than temporary. He turned, leaning across the kitchen counter to kiss her forehead.

'That doesn't mean… Last night was everything, Callie. You are so much more than beautiful.'

She smiled, as if that was just what she'd wanted to hear. 'I couldn't get enough of you.'

That was what *he* wanted to hear. Despite the feeling that the world had spun a little slower over the last twenty-four hours, he couldn't help wanting more.

'We have an hour before we need to leave. Ten

minutes to finish our coffee, and then twenty minutes to shower and dress….'

'Which means we'd have to be quick…' She grinned at him, taking a condom out of the pocket of his robe and holding it up. It was disconcerting the way she thought so much like him.

'That's thirty seconds you've saved already.' He rounded the kitchen counter swiftly, taking her toast out of her hand and putting it down on the plate. Picking her up off the stool, he carried her over to the sofa.

She was shrieking with laughter, wriggling in his arms, and when he tipped her down onto the cushions she made a lunge for him, pulling him down. This was how it had been all night, a heady give and take that they'd both revelled in.

'Not this time.' He pinned her down, grasping at her wrists with one hand and undoing the tie of the dressing gown with the other. 'This time's all for you…'

She stared into his gaze, suddenly still. The smile she gave, when she knew he was about to make love to her, had the power to break him. But having more of Callie, feeling her break him, was the one and only thing he wanted right now.

It wasn't just that every minute with Ben seemed like ten. Last night he actually *had* spent hours making love to her. And his idea of a quickie before they went to work was thirty minutes, dedicated to giving her an orgasm so devastating that she would have fallen off the sofa if she hadn't been safe in his arms.

It felt as if his scent were on her. Swirling around her in her car as she drove the longest route she could think of to the fire station, so that there would be no possibility of them arriving together. No one seemed to notice it when she joined the rest of the crew at the ready room table, making sure she sat with her back to Ben, but when she pulled her sweater over her head, draping it over the back of her chair, she shivered, sure that her shirt smelled of him.

It was just his washing powder. His soap on her skin. But still there was that indefinable extra element to it, which reminded her of Ben alone.

Perhaps she should go and do something useful, instead of awkwardly trying to pretend that he wasn't in the room. She grabbed her camera, standing up suddenly and almost cannoning into a wall of hard muscle.

'Oh… Sorry…' She jumped back in alarm, and Ben grabbed her arm to steady her.

'My fault. Are you okay?'

She glanced around the table, suddenly terrified that it would be obvious that they'd been making love less than two hours ago. If it was, no one seemed to care.

'Yes, I'm fine.'

He nodded, grinning. Then the pressure of his fingers tightened on her arm for a moment, before letting go. His lips formed a silent word, just for her, and then he turned away.

Later...

Later. Ben had kept himself busy tonight, and Callie had done the same, but that one word made all the difference. An acknowledgement that the last twenty-four hours couldn't just be forgotten now they were back at work. She wanted there to be a *later* too, even if it only meant half an hour alone to talk to him.

'Not another one...' Eve threw a half-eaten piece of stollen in the bin as the bell rang and Ben called out that this was their second abandoned car fire of the night. 'What is it with Boxing Day and joyriders? Haven't they ever heard of "Silent Night"?'

'That was supposed to be last night, wasn't it?' The night after Christmas Day.

'Is it? I suppose we're making up for it now, then.' Eve was already collecting her gear, ready to go. 'Good shot at four o'clock.'

The crew had taken to pointing out what they reckoned were good camera shots. Mostly Callie smiled and took the picture anyway, knowing she could delete it later, but Eve had a good eye. When she looked in the direction that Eve had indicated, she saw Ben, working with one of the other men to heave some heavy equipment onto the tender.

It was a great shot, full of movement and urgency. Callie raised her camera and then lowered it. She hadn't taken a picture of Ben all day, feeling that somehow it crossed the line between professional and personal.

He glanced over, catching her watching him, and grinned. And then he was back at work, making sure that the crew had everything they would need and calling out to Callie to get on the truck *now* if she was coming with them.

The night shift was finally over. Callie had looked for Ben in the small office and bumped into Eve her way back to the ready room.

'Have you seen Ben?'

'You wanted him? He's gone.'

'Gone...?' The news hit Callie with an uncomfortable force.

'Yes, he got a text and then dashed off. Said he had to see to something.' It seemed that some of the shock of realisation had shown on Callie's face, because Eve was looking at her questioningly. 'He'll be back here tonight. Or call him if it can't wait.'

'It can wait.' Callie forced herself to smile. 'Sleep well. I'll see you tonight.'

Callie collected up her gear, walking alone to her car. She'd been so sure that *later* had meant the end of their shift. Maybe she'd been mistaken. But Ben could have given her just one smile before rushing away. Just one sign that he hadn't come to regret what had happened between them. Callie grimly shook her head as she got into her car. It wasn't as if they'd promised each other anything.

All the same, Ben's scent seemed to follow her all the way home. She showered, throwing her clothes into the washing basket, and still it stayed with her like a ghost of Christmas, curling around her senses when she closed the curtains against the morning light and got into bed.

Callie had tried to sleep and found it impossible. Cocoa hadn't helped, and neither had sitting in front of the television, watching daytime TV. In the end, she had eventually fallen asleep for a short stretch on the sofa, and woken with a stiff neck. She considered staying at home tonight, but thought better of it. If Ben didn't want to say goodbye that was fine. She still had to say her goodbyes to the rest of the crew.

She was late, missing roll-call and Ben's briefing. She popped her head around the ready room door, letting the firefighters know that she was there, and then made for the locker room.

'You made it…' Ben's voice behind her made her jump.

'Yes. Sorry, I was a bit delayed.' She turned to him, trying not to look into his face.

Keep it professional. Get through tonight and then walk away.

'Since you're not officially on the roster, you're at liberty to come and go as you please.' He took a step closer, his voice quieter. 'I want to apologise. For last night.'

Callie's mouth felt suddenly dry. 'That's all right. You're at liberty to come and go as you please as well.'

'You've every right to be angry…'

'I'm *not* angry, Ben.

'Let me explain—'

Oh, no. Explanations weren't something that either of them had signed up for. Explanations made everything complicated.

'There's no need to explain anything. We're not…' She felt herself redden as the words she wanted wouldn't come.

'Not what?' He raised his arm, planting it against one of the locker doors. It was an unequivocal sign that if she wanted to end this conversation, she was going to have to push past him, and that would involve touching him.

'I'm nothing to you. You're nothing to me.'

The look he gave her made her into a liar. She wanted him so badly that he could be everything to her if he would just reach out and touch her.

'That's not true—' He broke off as the bell rang, cursing quietly under his breath.

'Go. You have to go.' She'd been saved. By an actual bell, of all things.

He turned, and relief flooded through her as Ben began to hurry away. But it took more than a bell to dissuade Ben.

'We're not done, Callie. Not yet…' He shot the words over his shoulder.

CHAPTER TEN

THEY *WERE* DONE. They had to be. They'd made love, and Callie had been hoping they might be friends. Maybe even lovers again, for a little while. But he'd walked away without a word, and that was something she couldn't deal with. Not when she'd been beginning to feel that she might just be able to depend on him.

It was a busy night again. There wasn't much time for photographs at the fire station, and when they were called out, Callie made sure that she took up the vantage point that Ben indicated, without looking at him. The crew's mood became silent and dogged, as if they were all wishing for the end of the shift as much as Callie was. This morning they could all go home and celebrate what was left of Christmas with their families.

When she said her goodbyes, trading hugs and promising not to be a stranger, Ben was nowhere to be seen. Callie emptied her locker and made for the car park.

He was leaning against her car, hands in the pockets of his jacket in the morning chill. Callie took a breath, trying not to alter her pace as she walked towards him.

'I'm off now. I'll see you around.' Callie had regretted her bitter words in the locker room earlier. There was no reason to be uncivilised about this.

'No, you won't. Not if you can help it, anyway.'

Right. So this was how he wanted it. 'Step aside, Ben. I'm going home.'

He moved silently away from the back door of the car, letting her open it and put her bag inside. Then suddenly he was there again, blocking her path to the driver's door.

'Ben!' Callie tried to inject as much warning as she could into her voice.

'Trust me, Callie. Just enough to come with me and let me explain.'

He knew that was impossible. He knew she couldn't trust.

But the look on his face told her that he wasn't going to give up. Callie puffed out a breath.

'All right. We'll go to the café on the corner and you can buy me a cup of tea.'

Ben had messed up. Big time. He'd been longing to see Callie alone, knowing from their quiet, exchanged smiles that she wanted to see him. And then his phone had pinged, and the text had sent him running for the hills. Scared and confused.

He owed her an apology, and an explanation. After that, she was at liberty to throw her tea in his face and tell him that he needed to get his act together, and that he couldn't treat people the way he'd just treated her. It was no less than he'd been telling himself all night.

She followed him wordlessly to the café. One of the few small cafés left in London, where just one kind of coffee was served, and you could get a traditional breakfast. The morning rush was over, and they could sit in one of the booths that were arranged along the side wall and get a little privacy.

He ordered tea, and coffee and a bacon sandwich for himself. Callie's beautiful eyes were studying him solemnly and they gave him the courage to broach a subject that he suddenly realised he'd kept secret from even his closest friends.

'I rushed off yesterday morning, because I had a text…' When he said it out loud the reason sounded even more flimsy.

'I know. Eve said.' She brushed it off as if it meant nothing, but the hurt in her eyes gave the lie to that. If he was going to make her understand, he had to tell her everything.

Show her everything. Ben took his phone from

his pocket, tapping the icon for messages and then displaying the four texts that had come in moments apart yesterday from an unrecognised number. When he laid the phone on the table in front of her, Callie ignored it.

'They all say the same thing. They're from my ex-partner.'

She puffed out a breath and looked at the phone, frowning when she saw the texts.

Happy Christmas. Love Isabel x

'Ben, if you wanted to be with someone else then you could have just said. The only promise we made to each other was that…there were no promises.'

'I didn't want to be with her—' He broke off as the waitress chose that moment to put their cups down in front of them, adding a plate of bacon sandwiches for Ben. He managed to get a 'Thank you' in before she turned her back on them, and then they were alone again.

Ben pushed the bacon sandwiches to one side. There was something he needed to do more than eat. More than breathe, if he was honest. 'It's a long story…'

'Not too long, I hope.' She glanced at her tea in a clear indication that when she'd drunk it she would be gone.

'I'll keep it as short as I can. Isabel and I met eighteen months ago, I know her brother slightly. We went out a few times, it was a pretty casual thing…'

'Because you don't do anything other than casual.' She shot him a cool glance.

'Things were different then. She was a lot of fun to be with, but it was never going to work between us. I said I'd like to see her again but just as a friend. Then I got this long rambling letter, saying that she knew I didn't mean it, and that she'd decided to take me back.'

'*Did* you mean it?'

'Yeah, I meant it. But the more I tried to step back, the more she seemed to cling to me. She said that it was only my shift patterns that were keeping us apart, and that she'd give up her job so we could be together.'

Callie took a gulp of her tea, concern registering in her face. Maybe she could already see the danger that Ben had failed to recognise at the time. 'I know shift work is hard on relationships but…most people find a way to work that out.'

She didn't know the half of it yet. 'I told her that neither of us were giving up our jobs, but she wouldn't take no for an answer. She started to write to me, cards and letters, two or three times a day. She called and texted me at work all the time, and in the end I had to block her number.

I reckoned she'd get tired of me soon enough if I didn't respond...'

Just talking about it was making Ben feel sick with self-loathing, but when he looked into Callie's face he saw a warmth he didn't deserve.

'In my experience, when a woman acts like that, they generally don't get tired of it. It's more likely to be a result of what's going on with her, not anything you did.'

It was good of her to make excuses for him, but Ben knew exactly what he'd done. When she heard everything, Callie would too, and she'd see that what had happened between them had been *his* fault, and maybe stop telling herself that the world had it in for her.

'When Isabel started calling on the landline at work, I realised that I had to do something. So I went to see her and told her that it couldn't go on. No more calls and no more letters. The next evening I came home from work to find a bunch of flowers and a note, saying that she wouldn't call again.'

'That's...' Callie shrugged. 'I'm guessing it wasn't a sign that she was beginning to find some boundaries?'

'The flowers were in a vase, sitting on the kitchen counter. She'd let herself in with a key I didn't know she had.'

The sick feeling, that had overwhelmed Ben when he'd looked at the flowers returned. In that moment he'd begun to understand violation. He'd thrown the flowers away, looking around the apartment for signs of Isabel, and he'd found them. Dismay had turned to despair as he'd slowly begun to realise that someone had been through everything he owned.

'You changed the locks. Please tell me you changed the locks.'

'It was late and I was working the following morning. I didn't have a chance. I texted Isabel to tell her that she wasn't to let herself in again and…the following evening I got home and found her in my bed. Naked. I told her that she had to get dressed and go, and she told me she was pregnant.'

Callie put her head in her hands, rubbing her face in a gesture of helplessness. Ben thought that he'd probably done exactly the same thing himself.

'I always wanted kids but I knew this wasn't an ideal situation to bring a child into. I told her that I'd take care of them both but that we couldn't go back to being a couple. Then, a couple of weeks later, Isabel told me she'd made a mistake and she never had been pregnant. I didn't know how to feel…'

It had been a mixture of relief and sorrow. Concern for Isabel, although in truth she hadn't seemed to mind all that much, and guilt. Ben had never felt so deeply flawed, and so incapable of doing anything about it.

'Ben…don't take this the wrong way, but did it occur to you that she was just trying to make you stay with her?'

Callie had asked the question that Ben hadn't dared to even think. 'When a woman tells you she's pregnant and the baby's yours, disbelieving her isn't the best way to respond.'

'Yes, I know, but…' She puffed out a breath. 'You had to know that this wasn't normal.'

'I tried to get her some help, but she wouldn't take it. The next thing I knew I had a call from her brother, saying she'd locked herself in her flat and was threatening to take a full packet of paracetamol.'

Callie was shaking her head slowly. 'She needed professional help. Lots of it… He didn't call the emergency services?'

'Isabel was asking for me. I went round and broke the door down. As far as I could see, she hadn't taken anything, but we took her to A and E just to be sure. She fought me and said she wanted to die…' Ben closed his eyes. Isabel had kicked and screamed, blackening his eye. In the end, that had turned out to be the only physical injury in a night that had taken a heavy emotional toll on everyone.

'She got the help she needed, though?'

'Yes. Her brother and I both stayed the night to keep an eye on her, and the counsellor I'd contacted agreed to see her the next day. He told me that it was best if I didn't have any further involvement, and that I should let him and her family give her the support she needed.'

'So that was it?'

'I speak to her brother regularly. He says she's doing well.'

'And these texts...' Callie nudged his phone with one finger. 'I imagine it was really hard to see them.'

Somehow Ben managed to smile. 'Yes. I called her brother and he says they're dealing with it.'

'But you can't help.' Callie turned the corners of her mouth down. 'That's pretty tough for someone like you, who's used to making a difference.'

She made him realise what really hurt. The helplessness, and his complete inability to make things right.

'It's the best way. Maybe she really did just want to wish me a happy Christmas...' Ben shrugged. 'But that doesn't matter. I want to tell you that the way I acted yesterday morning had nothing to do with you. And that I'm sorry.'

'I imagine it was a knee-jerk reaction.' She was looking straight into his eyes now. 'A bit like the one I had.'

'You had every right to be upset.'

'Don't make excuses for me.' She reached forward, picking up one of the bacon sandwiches from his plate. 'Have you talked about this with anyone?'

Ben shook his head. If he had then maybe he'd have found the perspective and understanding that Callie was so ready to give. Or maybe that wouldn't have made such a difference if it hadn't come from her.

'Maybe you should.' She reached out, taking his hand. 'Stop trying to pack it away in a box and forget about it.'

How did she know him so well, after so little time? Callie seemed to get the parts of him that even he didn't get.

He picked up the other half of the sandwich and they ate in silence. There was something about the silence between him and Callie. Warm and companionable, it was allowing them both to heal.

'Are we done, Callie?' Finally he found it in himself to speak.

'I...' She looked up at him, and he saw all the warmth in her eyes that he'd found when he'd made love to her. 'No. We're not done yet.'

CHAPTER ELEVEN

CALLIE HAD FOLLOWED Ben's car back to his apartment, and they stood quietly together in the old, creaking lift. Her heart had gone out to him when she'd seen the pain and guilt in his face when he'd talked about Isabel. He'd been damaged...

But, then, she was damaged too. And somehow that meant that they fitted together well. There was no danger that either of them would take this relationship beyond what the other could handle.

Ben opened the door to his apartment, ushering her inside. Light was streaming through the high windows, making the ornaments on the tree glisten and gleam. Christmas wasn't over yet.

Neither were they. Callie reached for him, and he moved suddenly, taking her into his arms, his warmth flooding through her and making her gasp. His keys clattered unheeded on the floor and he backed her against the wall, his hand behind her head to cushion it from the exposed bricks.

'I have the next four days off. Will you spend them with me?' He kissed the soft skin behind her ear, and Callie shivered.

'That would be...wonderful.'

Tired from the night's work, they'd spent the rest of the day and the following night sleeping and making love. And when dawn had broken, Ben had got out of bed, promising her breakfast. Sausages, bacon, eggs...the works.

'That smells great.' Callie had put on her clothes, fresh from the washer-dryer, and had gone downstairs to find him standing at the cooker, wearing a towelling robe. 'You know the good thing about you is that you always have a full fridge.'

He leaned over, kissing her. 'The only good thing?'

'You know the others. I'm not going to repeat myself.'

'Okay. Will you watch the pan while I go and take a shower? I might be a while, I'll be needing to revive my broken ego.' He flashed her an irresistible grin and Callie laughed.

'Your ego's just fine....' She called after him.

He reappeared in a pair of worn jeans and a crisp white T-shirt. Crisp and white suited him.

It accentuated his dark hair and the softly smouldering look in his eyes.

'Why don't we go to the zoo this afternoon? I haven't been to Regent's Park in ages.' He crowded her away from the pan and Callie took two mugs from the cupboard to make the coffee.

'Sounds like a plan. I like the zoo. I'd like to pop home this morning and get a change of clothes.' Something a bit nicer than work boots and trousers perhaps.

'Okay. Leave your camera behind so that I know you'll come back.'

Callie laughed, winding her arms around his waist. 'I'll be back. I'll leave my tablet as well, so you can have a look through the photos if you like.'

He turned away from the pan to face her. 'Really? You told me that I was the last person on the list to get a look at them.'

'I was making a point. Everyone has to approve the photographs that feature them, but it doesn't matter if you take a look. I'd really like to hear your thoughts, actually.' They'd come so far since that first day.

'Ah. So you were putting me in my place, were you?'

'Only because you didn't want me around.'

He bent down, kissing her. 'I can't imagine what I was thinking. I must have been crazy.'

'I thought you were nice looking with a bit of an attitude.'

'I thought you were gorgeous. But very scary.' Ben wound one of her curls around his finger. She knew he liked it better when she left it to curl naturally, and letting her defences down with Ben was becoming surprisingly easy.

They tramped all the way round Regent's Park, working up an appetite for lunch, before going to the zoo. They then spent the evening curled up on the sofa together, watching an old film, and then another night together. Ben was sure that there must be something in his life that had made him as happy as Callie did, but he couldn't call it to mind.

They got up early and went out for breakfast, then took a stroll through the buzzing network of streets of the East End to do a little window shopping. Now Callie was sitting cross-legged on the sofa, wearing an oversized sweater and a flowered skirt, which draped around her legs. She was busy with a pad and pencil, listing and ticking off photographs. And Ben was busy watching her.

'So...you have a thing about fire engines, then? Or is it firefighters?'

She looked up at him, grinning. 'You're the

one with the thing for shiny red and chrome. And I only have a thing for *one* firefighter.'

Ben chuckled. Callie had a way of making him feel good without really trying. 'What made you propose this project at the fire station, then? I imagine you could get much better rates elsewhere, and you're putting a lot of work into it.'

'Actually, I'm doing it free.' Her cheeks reddened, as if she'd been caught in a good deed and was slightly embarrassed about it.

'Really? So what made you do it?'

In the last two days they'd talked about everything, felt everything together. It seemed so natural to ask questions but this one made Callie hesitate for a moment.

'I want to make a difference with my photography, not just take good pictures. I think it's important to show the realities of the work the emergency services do.'

Ben suspected there was a little more to it than that. 'I would have thought the ambulance service would be closer to your heart.'

'I particularly wanted to come to a fire station because...of my dad. You take risks every day in the course of your work, and I wanted to understand that a little better.'

Something prickled at the back of Ben's neck. As if a door had just swung open, and he wasn't sure whether he wanted to go through it.

'And do you?'

She shrugged. 'Maybe. I heard everything you said about the choices you made, and I understand it. It's a bit soon to be feeling it, though.'

It was almost a relief to imagine the door swinging shut again. The possibilities behind it, what might happen if Callie found a place where she could contemplate a long-term relationship with a certain firefighter, weren't something that Ben had thought about.

Callie had gone back to her list now, clearly not inclined to say any more. Ben should concentrate on the here and now and make the most of that, not worry about an impossible future.

'You fancy some lunch? I'd really like to see the photographs you've chosen, and perhaps we could do that afterwards over a glass of wine.'

She nodded. Risk averted. 'Yes, thanks. That would be nice.'

Callie was happy with her choice. Two or three photographs for each month, featuring different aspects of the work. Some formal and others informal, with a flavour of the Christmas festivities at the fire station on the December page.

'I like these especially.' Ben pointed to the choice for November. 'Putting the one of Eve with Isaac right next to the one of her on duty makes them both stronger.'

He'd picked the ones she was most pleased with. 'I like them too.'

'You know, if you want to make a difference, you could think about doing more of this. You have a way of showing strength and beauty that could change lives.'

Callie hadn't thought of it that way before. 'Portraiture as therapy, you mean? That would be…amazing.'

'I think so too.' He grinned, putting his hand to his chest in a gesture of mock distress. 'Although I'm mortified to find that you no longer see me as either strong *or* beautiful.'

He'd noticed. Out of the hundreds of photographs she'd taken during the last two shifts at the fire station, there wasn't a single one of Ben. Callie tried to laugh it off.

'Sleeping with you and then taking photos… It didn't seem right somehow.' Callie had never *wanted* to take photographs of anyone she'd slept with. Giving that much of herself and then having the photograph to prove it after it was over didn't much appeal to her.

Ben nodded, not seeming to want to push the subject. But she could see that he was a little disappointed with her answer. And so was Callie. They'd been talking about giving her heart to her photography, and she'd shied away from the first opportunity.

She looked around the apartment. Ben was so perfect, so handsome that she wanted something imperfect to photograph him against.

'Do you have any more exposed brickwork? Like that?' Callie pointed up at the roof space, spanned by heavy metal beams and flanked on either side by bare bricks.

'I have plenty of exposed brickwork, if that's what you want.' He laid the tablet down on the sofa between them, reaching for the soft sheepskin boots that she'd slipped off and left by the sofa. 'You'll have to put those on, though.'

'Where are we going?' Callie pulled the boots on, reaching for her camera and a folding tripod from her bag. He didn't answer, getting to his feet and leading the way to the doorway under the stairs. It led to a small corridor where the spare bedroom was situated, and then another door that Callie had assumed must be a cupboard. When he unlocked it and swung it open, the chill of a large, unheated space brushed her cheek.

Ben flipped a switch and lights came on, pooling under metal shades. The floor area was almost as much again as that of the apartment, and the space was clearly a continuation of it, double height with a cavernous roof supported by the same metal beams. But it was entirely untouched, bare brick walls and metal window frames, caked with many layers of paint.

'What's this, Ben?'

'When I chose the space I wanted I thought that it would be good to have room to grow, if I ever needed it.' He shrugged diffidently, as if he didn't know now why *room to grow* had ever been a factor in his thinking.

Callie swallowed hard. This was the family home that Ben had once wanted but now couldn't contemplate having. If she'd crossed a line, by taking her camera out and trying to capture what he meant to her, then he'd crossed one too, by bringing her here.

Ben hadn't brought anyone else in here for over a year. He no longer had any need of the space that he'd once thought might accommodate the needs of a family.

He loved his apartment. Even if he didn't grow old here, he'd reckoned on growing a good bit older. But however old he got, he reckoned that this space would remain the same, ready for the next owner to make something of it.

Watching Callie taking photographs of the walls and windows calmed him a little. She saw it in terms of light and shade, texture and colour. It was just bricks and mortar to her.

'Over there...' She'd set the camera onto the

tripod she'd brought with her and suddenly turned her attention to him, pointing to a stretch of wall by one of the high windows.

'Here?' Ben walked over to the wall, feeling suddenly awkward and under scrutiny.

'No, a couple of yards to your left. Closer to the window… That's good. Maybe just rest your hand on the windowsill.'

Every time Callie pointed the camera at him, his hands became suddenly clumsy and felt twice their usual size. At least he knew what to do with one of them now and he complied, feeling the chill of the tiled sill under his fingers.

She bent to adjust the lens, and he smiled in response. Being photographed was far easier when Callie just crept up on you and you weren't aware of it.

'Okay… You're a little wooden…' She wrinkled her nose, inspecting her camera as if adjusting the settings might make him feel more at ease. Ben waited and saw her face light up as she looked towards him again. 'Oh. Look.'

She pointed at the window and he turned. It was snowing, large flakes blowing against the window and already gathering at the bottom of the small panes of glass. He heard her boots, padding softly on the concrete floor, and felt her body next to his.

'It's lovely, isn't it?' She stared up into the

dark sky. This was clearly one of those things that Callie just wanted to experience, rather than photograph.

'Yes, it is.' He took her in his arms. It would be...interesting...to make love with her here. Feel the cold of her hands on his skin, while heat exploded between them. It wouldn't be comfortable, but feeling the rough brickwork against his back, protecting her against it with his own body, seemed only to heighten the pleasure of the fantasy.

It *was* just a fantasy. Callie wasn't his to protect, and even doing it for a while would make him want what he was too afraid to take. Her presence made him realise that a few of his old dreams still lingered here, not yet banished with the ruthlessness that he'd swept them out of the other parts of his life.

She walked away from him, clearly set on the idea of photographing him and not the snow. Ben resumed his awkward-feeling pose, looking at the camera.

'Don't smile.' Her voice floated out from behind the lens and he pulled his face straight. She took a couple of photographs, but seemed unhappy with them.

'Look at me, Ben. Think about...the wall behind your back. How does it feel?'

'It feels...like a wall.'

'Okay. That's a start. How does the window feel?'

'It feels a little draughty.' Ben grinned at her. 'I don't have your ability to give walls and windows any more meaning than just...'

He broke off. Callie had stepped forward again, standing on her toes to kiss him. When he moved his hand to wind it around her waist she stopped him.

'Don't move…. Don't move.'

'You do this with all your portraits?'

'It's a new technique. Just for you.'

Ben liked that a lot. And he liked the way it was difficult to keep still while Callie planted her palms on his chest, kissing him. The way she pressed herself against his body, seeming to know that he was suddenly aching for her.

Hot and cold. The rough surface of the wall against his back and the softness of her skin. It was almost unbearable.

'Stay still.' She backed away from him, her gaze still locked with his. Her fingers moved to her lips, grazing them as if she was trying to recreate the feel of his mouth. 'Still…'

He felt it. The way that Callie brought emotion and meaning into everyday actions and things. The way she wove a fantasy into the hard facts of reality. As he gazed into her eyes, he was aware of nothing other than her.

She must have stretched out her hand and touched the camera, because suddenly she walked back towards him. 'I think I've got the shots I want.'

He wound his arms around her. Ben was still trembling slightly from an emotion that he couldn't quite describe. Whatever shot she'd taken, he imagined that it must show both their hearts, and he wasn't sure whether he could bear to see it. He'd told her that he liked the rawness of her photographs, but maybe this was a little too raw.

'It's cold in here.' It was the only excuse he could think of to move. Callie nodded, breaking away from him, collecting the camera and tripod as he ushered her back into the apartment, closing the door behind them and locking it. The lines that they'd promised not to cross had somehow been crossed, and the feeling that maybe they'd gone too far nagged at him.

'You want to see?' Callie had fitted the lead from her tablet to the camera, and the photographs had already downloaded.

'I'm…not sure.'

'I can delete them.' She turned her mouth down, seeming to sense his discomfiture.

'No…' Ben held out his hand. How bad could it be? A regular guy, standing against a wall.

She walked over to the hearth, warming herself, while Ben looked through the photos. It was all there. His face, his eyes were just the same as the ones he saw in the mirror every morning, but there was a raw undertone of passion.

The shadows, the texture of the brickwork and the smooth white of his T-shirt. Snow falling at the window and warmth in his face. It was a mass of inconsistencies, which felt rather too uncomfortably like the truth.

He laid the tablet down on the sofa and walked across to the fire. 'They're great. You have a talent, Callie. Don't let it go to waste.'

She snuggled into his arms. The screen on the tablet dimmed and then shut down, but Ben couldn't shake the image in his head.

That night, Ben made love to her tenderly, almost regretfully. Callie woke in the early hours to find him lying on his back, staring at the ceiling, and when he realised that she was awake he turned over, curling his body around hers and whispering to her to go back to sleep.

In the morning, she woke to the sounds of him moving around downstairs. She stumbled into the shower, rubbing her face hard in the stream of water, trying to gather her splintered thoughts.

They'd stepped out of the bounds that they'd both set themselves and tried to touch the impossible. And the bond that had formed so naturally between them couldn't withstand that.

Callie closed her eyes, turning her face up into the stream of water. If they called it a day now, they could keep everything that was special. Carrying on would only destroy that, because at some point they'd find that their deeply held fears were stronger than their desire to be together.

She blow-dried her hair, tugging it straight. Then she dressed and packed her things away in her overnight bag.

He had coffee ready for her, along with toast and apricot preserve. The silence grew heavier by the minute.

'I think…' He broke off, realising that Callie had opened her mouth to speak at the same time as he had. Even in this, they seemed in perfect synchronicity. 'You first.'

'I should go home. I have some more work to do on the photos, and I need my computer and printer.'

He nodded. 'Yeah. There are a few things I need to do today too. Call into the fire station maybe…'

This was the final acknowledgement that it was over between them. Irretrievably broken. Callie didn't have to go home any more than he needed to go to the station. After all the honesty they'd shared, they'd started to make excuses to each other.

'Right, then. It's been…'

'It's been too good to last.' The sudden flash of warmth in his eyes was too much to bear, and Callie looked away. She gulped the rest of her coffee down and put her mug in the sink, then collected up her camera and tablet, stowing them away in her camera bag.

'I'll walk you to your car.' Ben picked up his keys, shoving them into the pocket of his jeans.

'No, thank you. I'd rather you didn't.' Callie pulled on her coat and turned to face him. 'Time to get back to our real lives. Live yours well, Ben.'

'You too, Callie.'

She was aware that he stayed in the doorway after the lift had creaked its way up to collect her and she'd got in. As it crept slowly downwards, she heard his front door close. Callie took a deep breath, trying to stop herself from trembling.

It was done. They'd both lived up to their side of the bargain and the whole of the rest of her life was waiting for her. Somehow the rest of her life seemed an awfully long time to contemplate at the moment.

Ben was sure that this was the right thing to do. There was no way forward, he'd understood that last night when he'd showed Callie the other side of the apartment.

Christmas had been a fantasy bubble, where neither of them had needed to think about the difficulties and complications of real life. They'd been able to live for the moment, and that was why it had all tasted so intoxicatingly good. But if every day of the year was Christmas Day, the novelty of it would soon wear thin.

He watched her go for as long as he dared. Until the lift began to move downwards and he could no longer see her behind the metal trellis of the gates. Then he kept the promise he'd made and turned away. He would miss her, but this was what they both needed.

CHAPTER TWELVE

THE DULL THROB of missing Ben hadn't eased off in over six weeks. Callie knew that she couldn't contemplate anything other than a parting, and neither could he, but that didn't seem to make things any better. But if she thought *that* was bad, there was worse to follow.

'How was your day?' Sophie, her best friend at the hospital, was sitting in the canteen, a cup of tea in front of her. They'd followed this routine for years, meeting up for half an hour after work every Thursday, whenever their shifts allowed. This Thursday the normality of it was comforting.

'Busy. Have you seen a red-haired boy? Acid burns to his stomach?'

Sophie nodded. 'Yes, he came up onto the ward at lunchtime. You brought him in?'

'Yes. How is he?'

'The burns are second degree. The doctor had a look at him and said that he doesn't need a skin graft. It'll be a while but he'll heal. How did a five-year-old manage to get burns like that?'

'Bottle of bleach under the sink. His mother said that she never screwed the lid back on properly because she couldn't get it open again when she wanted to use it.'

Sophie rolled her eyes. 'Great. Because the whole point of child-proof containers is for so-called adults to leave them open.'

'Something like that. I don't think she'll be doing it again.'

'Bit bloody late now...' Sophie's blue eyes flashed with anger and Callie nodded.

'Yeah. Keep an eye on him for me, won't you? He's a brave kid.'

Sophie nodded. This was what they did. Talked a little and got the frustrations of a day's work out of their systems. Then Sophie went home to her husband, and Callie went home to...

Another worried, sleepless night. It was about time she grasped the nettle and found out, one way or the other.

'You want one of these?' Sophie pulled a packet of blueberry muffins out of her bag, and offered one to Callie.

'No, thanks. Feeling a bit sick.'

'Oh. Stomach bug?'

'No, I don't think so. I've been feeling like this for more than a week.'

'Probably not something you've eaten, then.' Sophie frowned. 'You're a bit young to be getting an ulcer, but it might be stress...'

'It's not stress.'

Sophie rolled her eyes. 'You don't always know it, these things creep up on you. So what do *you* think it is, then?'

'It's...worse in the mornings.' That should be enough of a clue. By now Callie's mother would have been on her way to the shops to buy wool to knit a pair of bootees.

'Worse in the mornings? If it's acid reflux, you really should go and see someone about that.' Sophie took a sip of tea.

Maybe it was a bit much to expect of Sophie. Callie had been like a rabbit caught in the headlights, immobilised and too afraid to do anything to either confirm or deny her increasing suspicions. Wanting her friend to step in and sweep her off on a tide of common sense when she didn't have all the facts wasn't entirely fair.

'I have amenorrhoea, nausea in the mornings and my breasts are a little swollen and tender.'

Sophie stared at her, her teacup suspended at a precarious angle in mid-air. 'You're pregnant?'

Finally! 'Well, I don't know for sure... Don't spill your tea.'

Callie grabbed the cup and set it down on the table. Sophie was still wide-eyed, obviously trying to decide which question to ask first.

'You haven't taken a test?' Her friend came through for her, asking just the question that Callie wanted her to ask.

'No, I… I was too afraid.'

Sophie's nursing training kicked in. Grabbing her coat and bag from the back of her chair and taking hold of Callie's hand, she marched her to the door of the canteen. 'You're coming with me. Now.'

They drove to Sophie's house, stopping on the way for a visit to the chemist. Jeff, Sophie's husband, greeted Callie warmly, asking if she was staying for dinner, and Sophie bundled him into the kitchen while Callie sat miserably on the sofa. Then she heard the front door bang shut.

'Jeff's gone to the pub.' Sophie appeared in the doorway of the sitting room, the paper bag from the chemist in her hand.

'Soph, I'm sorry. I didn't mean…'

'That's all right. It's quiz night, and his mates will be down there. Do you want a glass of water?'

'No, thanks. I think I'm good.'

'Right.' Sophie jerked her thumb towards the stairs. 'Come on.'

* * *

Callie handed the wand from the pregnancy test kit around the bathroom door without even looking at it. She heard Sophie walking downstairs and filled the basin, splashing water on her face, before following her back to the sitting room. Sophie waited for her to sit down and then glanced at the wand again, as if to confirm what she'd seen.

'You're pregnant. It says more than three weeks.' Sophie's voice was calm. That was good, Callie needed some calm.

'Right. Thanks.'

'Do you know when it happened? Was there a contraceptive failure?'

'I don't remember there being one. We used condoms... I left it to him.' She'd let herself rely on Ben. 'I'm so stupid.'

'Let's get one thing straight here, Callie. These things happen. Not often, but abstinence is the only thing that's one hundred percent and beating yourself up about it isn't going to help.'

Callie shrugged. 'Oh, so tempting, though.'

'I know. But only you would give yourself a hard time over finding a reliable guy and leaving it to him to take care of things. You're still with him?'

'No, it's over. We were together between Christmas and the New Year.'

'When you were doing the shoot for the calendar?' Sophie's eyebrows shot up. 'He's a fireman?'

'Firefighter's the correct term…' Callie felt numb. She was pregnant by a man who didn't want to see her again.

'Not in this case. It's clearly a fire*man*.' Sophie stood, plumping herself down next to Callie on the sofa, putting her arms around her shoulders. 'I'm reckoning you haven't told anyone yet. Not your mum?'

'No. You know what Mum's like, she'll think it's all a case of cherubs and wedding bells.'

'You've got a point.' Sophie pressed her lips together. 'You need to tell him.'

Callie shook her head. 'I can do this by myself.'

'Yes, you can. Doesn't mean you should.' Sophie pulled Callie into a tight hug. 'You have choices here, Callie.'

'Thanks, Soph.' Callie could feel tears pricking at the corners of her eyes.

'No problem. You've always got me, you know that, don't you?'

Callie cried a little, clinging to Sophie. Then Sophie made a cup of tea, putting an unnecessary amount of sugar into Callie's cup. Callie appreciated the gesture, even though despair was a more accurate description of her reaction than shock.

'So…have you thought about what you'll do?' Sophie finally asked the question, her tone gentle.

'I'm keeping it.' There had never been any question in Callie's mind about that.

'Good. What about work?'

'I don't want to give up medicine. But I've been thinking about developing my photography, maybe specialising in hospital settings or using it therapeutically.'

Sophie nodded. 'It would be good to have the option to work from home. And it's a great idea. What made you think of it?'

'Someone suggested it to me.' It had been Ben. It seemed that during their few days together he'd touched almost every part of her life. 'I don't know if it's viable.'

'If that's what you want to do then we'll find out. We'll read up on it, and I bet that Dr Lawrence, in the burns unit, would be able to advise you.'

'Thanks Soph. I don't know what I would have done without you.'

Sophie chuckled. 'You're usually the one who knows what to do in any given situation. You've seen me through a few scary times in my life, and I'm glad to return the favour.'

Callie sighed. 'I have to do this right. I'm the one responsible for this baby, and it's going to have a stable, secure childhood.'

'Not like yours, you mean.' Sophie pressed her lips together. 'Callie I know you don't want to hear this, but it is possible to find a man who'll step up and take care of you.'

'That's…complicated.'

'I've got time. I'd say I had a bottle of red in the kitchen but that's not much use at the moment.'

'Don't let me stop you. Have you got anything to eat?'

'You're hungry?' Sophie grinned. 'That's good. I've got some pasta and I'll make a Bolognese sauce. I'll drink for both of us while I'm cooking.'

'So…he's as much of a commitment-phobe as you are.' Sophie paused to stir the sauce and take a swig from her glass. 'Who knew that there were two of you?'

Callie smiled. Sophie had a way of making everything seem better, and she was beginning to feel that she might be equal to whatever was coming next.

'Well, it seemed a perfect fit at the time.'

'I'm sure it did. Which month is he in the calendar?' Sophie had already seen the photographs that Callie had taken, and her choices for the various months.

'He's one of the September ones.'

'September... September...' Sophie clicked her fingers, obviously trying to remember which photos Callie had selected for September. 'September! Mr Blue Eyes?'

'Yes.'

'You never said you slept with Mr Blue Eyes! Is he as gorgeous as the photo, or did you do something to it?'

'I don't airbrush my photos. He's...' More gorgeous. Callie swallowed down the thought, because that was only going to lead to heartbreak.

Sophie shook her head. 'All right, that's probably a bit too much information. Is he someone you'd want to be a father to your baby?'

'I can't tell him...' Callie felt a new, different panic start to overwhelm her.

'Don't you think he *should* know? At least give him the chance...'

'It's not that simple, Soph. His ex-girlfriend told him she was pregnant after they split up.'

'The one you said stalked him? He has a child with her?'

'After Ben told her that he'd look after her and the baby, but they couldn't be a couple, she said she'd made a mistake and that she wasn't pregnant after all.' Sophie's eyebrows shot up and Callie shrugged in answer to her unspoken question.

'I don't know, Soph. It didn't sound all that believable to me, but he's too honourable to say so. He said he knew the situation wasn't ideal, but he'd always wanted children and he was really upset when she told him she wasn't pregnant.'

Sophie thought for a moment. 'To be honest with you, Callie, if you were going to choose a father for your child, he doesn't sound like a bad bet. I know you grew up without your dad, but at least you know who he was. And this guy's honourable, and he wants kids...'

'That's just the problem, though. Suppose he does all the right things, and we get back together for the baby's sake. It didn't last at Christmas, and there's no reason why it should be any different next time around.' The only thing worse than not having Ben would be having him again and then losing him.

'Well...maybe make it clear that a relationship between you two isn't on the table. Tell him that it's just a matter of him knowing his child.'

'I suppose so.' It would be hard, but Callie could do it. For the sake of her child, she could do almost anything. 'I think... I'm going to leave it a little while, though. Until I'm more sure.'

'You mean until you're showing? So there's

no question in his mind that you actually *are* pregnant?'

Callie nodded. It would remove one of the difficulties, and it would give her plenty of time to think about what she was going to say to Ben.

CHAPTER THIRTEEN

Six months later

BEN HAD THOUGHT he'd caught a glimpse Callie. The woman had been sitting in the passenger seat of a car that had parked across the road to the entrance to his apartment building. He'd cursed himself roundly as he'd thought he'd stopped seeing her face in crowds and catching her scent when no one was there.

Maybe he shouldn't have ignored the text Callie had sent last month. Maybe he should have agreed to see her again, just once more, to lay the ghosts to rest. But Ben knew that it wasn't going to work that way. Seeing Callie again would just re-set the clock on the process of trying to forget her. Nothing had changed, and their ending would be exactly the same.

He entered his apartment, slinging his jacket onto the back of the nearest chair and opening a few windows so that a breeze would begin to circulate. It had been a long night, and this morning all he wanted to do was take a shower, then eat something and go to bed.

Ben heard the tap on his door as he walked back downstairs to the kitchen. Wondering who it was, he ran his hand through his wet hair to tidy it a bit and opened the door.

For a moment he wondered whether he *was* seeing ghosts. Her corn-blonde hair was curling softly around her face now, instead of being blow-dried straight. The image of the woman he'd slept with kicked him hard in the gut, only to be followed a split second later with a blow that almost brought him to his knees. She wasn't just pregnant. She was *very* pregnant.

'Callie…!'

'Hi. I rang the bell downstairs and someone let me in.' Her hand fluttered nervously to her stomach.

'I was in the shower.' As if it mattered. But the conversation seemed to be continuing under its own steam, while Ben's mind screamed in disbelief.

'I'm sorry if this isn't a convenient time.' Her gaze was clear-eyed and determined. A stab of guilt accompanied the thought that he really should have answered her text.

'It's…it's fine. I'm off shift now for three days.'

She nodded. 'I know. I looked up the rota on the fire station's website.'

Ben hadn't been aware that the watch rotas were even published on the website. But, then, he never had much occasion to visit it. Callie had obviously carefully picked her time to come here, perhaps reckoning that he might need a couple of days off work to get over the shock.

Shock. That was it. That was why he was standing there gawping at her and thinking about websites when there were far more important things to consider. It was why his limbs felt that they'd lost the power of movement. He needed to pull himself together.

'Please. Come in.' He stepped back from the doorway, watching her as she walked inside. She wore leggings and a pair of trainers, with a light summer top that fell loose over her stomach, reaching down to her hips. Pretty and practical. Less guarded somehow than the image she'd clung to when…

When he'd had sex with her. *He'd had sex with her and now she was pregnant.* The idea that the latter might well be a direct consequence of the former screamed in his head.

'How are you?' She looked up at him. Her gaze was less guarded too.

'Fine. Good.' The thoughts crowding his head seemed to have left him unable to frame a longer sentence. Ben took a breath, making an effort to at least say something.

'Come and sit down. Would you like a cup of tea or some juice?'

'Some juice would be great, if you have it.' Callie walked over to the breakfast bar and clambered up onto a high stool, exerting a little more effort in doing so that he remembered. Before he turned away from her to open the fridge door, he caught a glimpse of her drawing something out of her handbag. Ben poured two glasses of juice and when he turned back to face her she pushed a folded sheet of paper across the counter towards him.

'Since there's an elephant in the room, and I appear to be it...' She gave him a smile, as if she understood that he was struggling. 'As you can probably see, I'm going to have a baby. It was conceived in late December, here's my due date from the prenatal clinic.'

'Just tell me, Callie. Is the baby mine? Ours...' Finally. He'd managed to say something that sounded vaguely like the right thing.

'Yes. There's no doubt. But I want you to be sure too. There's no question you can't ask me.'

Where to start? 'Why...did you wait this long? Before you told me?'

She pressed her lips together. Clearly some questions were harder to answer than others.

'At first I wanted to be sure. Then I wanted to think things through a little. Time got away from me...'

She'd been afraid. Afraid to tell him, in case he didn't believe her. Or he told her he wanted nothing to do with the baby. Ben didn't quite know what he wanted at the moment, but he was sure of two things. If Callie said that this was his baby, he believed her. And if it was his baby, he wanted to be a father to it.

'We should—'

'Don't!' Her tone was almost sharp, and she gave a nervous smile. 'There's no *we*, Ben. I came to tell you this because you have a right to know. I don't expect anything from you, and I know it's a shock so I don't want you to say anything before you've thought about it.'

Yes, it was a shock. And the greatest shock of all was the way that his heart was pounding with joy at the thought that Callie was pregnant with *his* child. The way he wanted to take her in his arms and protect her. Now. From whatever threat he could think of.

He took a gulp of juice from his glass. It didn't surprise him all that much that Callie had a plan, and right now he wanted to know what that was. Needed to know whether he had some part in it.

'It's the last thing I thought would happen,

but…that doesn't mean that I'm not here for you, Callie.'

She nodded. 'It's your choice, Ben. I won't stop you from being involved with your child if that's what you want.'

Callie had clearly already ruled out the possibility of a relationship between them, and he could live with that. He had done for the last eight months. But this… This changed everything.

She drained her glass and started to wriggle uncertainly towards the edge of the stool. Ben rounded the counter, taking her arm and helping her down.

'Thanks.' She accepted his help but as soon as her feet were on the floor she moved away from him, delving into her bag and withdrawing another sheet of paper. 'This is my address and my phone number. When you've thought about things a bit, you can give me a call.'

'You're going?'

'It's probably best to leave you to think about this.'

She was right. He should marshal his thoughts before he said anything else, but the one thing he wanted her to know was that he'd be there for her.

'Tomorrow afternoon. May I come and see you then?'

'Tomorrow afternoon's fine. Does about two o'clock suit you?'

'Two it is. I'll be there.'

She nodded, making her way to the door. The sudden feeling that she couldn't—mustn't—go just yet seized Ben. 'How are you getting home now?'

'I came with a friend. She's waiting outside in the car.'

'Right. Well…be safe, Callie.'

She grinned at him. 'I always am. I'll see you tomorrow.'

'Wait…' She'd got almost to the door before Ben realised that there was one more piece of information that he had to know. 'Do you know whether it's a boy or a girl?'

'Yes. You'd like to know?'

'It doesn't make any difference to the way I feel but… Yes, I'd like to know.'

'It's a girl.'

She refused to allow him to see her downstairs and almost glared at him when he stood at the doorway, watching her into the lift. Ben waited until she'd disappeared from view before closing the door. Walking over to the sofa, he threw himself down on the cushions before his legs decided to give way.

He had a little more than twenty-four hours to get his act together. Ben stared up at the ceiling, too shell-shocked for anything other than one thought.

Callie was having *his* child. His daughter.

Callie was shaking. She'd made the step. *I'll do it tomorrow* had finally turned into *I'll do it today* and it hadn't been as bad as she'd expected it to be. She'd made her intentions clear, and Ben hadn't questioned whether he was the father of her baby. Maybe that would come later, after he'd thought about it a bit.

His car drew up outside her house at exactly two o'clock. It was something of a relief that he wasn't late. Callie had been sitting watching the road for the last half-hour, and she didn't think she could take much more of this. She watched him get out, and to her horror he reached back into the car, bringing out a bunch of flowers.

He didn't get it. This wasn't about flowers or promises. It was all about working out something that they could both live with long term, and having the gumption to stick with it. You didn't bring flowers to a business meeting, and Callie was determined to take the emotion out and be businesslike about this. She could think more clearly when she wasn't fantasising about his touch.

She took a deep breath as she walked to the door. Ben looked like a nervous suitor on a first date. He was wearing a tie and holding the flowers as if they were some kind of defensive measure.

At least they weren't roses. He proffered the bright yellow and orange blooms and she took them. She supposed that putting them in water would give her something to do with her hands, rather than clasping them together, her nails digging into her palms.

'How are you?' he enquired solicitously.

'Good, thank you.' If you didn't count the light-headedness and the constant feeling that she was about to be sick. That had been bugging her for a day or so now, and was probably more to do with Ben than her pregnancy.

'Have you just moved in here?' He was looking around the freshly painted hallway, and his gaze lit on the stack of mover's crates under the stairs.

'Yes, I…was thinking of selling my flat and getting a small house, and this place came up. It didn't seem quite the right time to be moving but it was too good to miss.'

'And you've been decorating?' There was a trace of reproach in his tone.

'I haven't been doing it myself. The last owner had a penchant for primary colours, which is probably why he had a problem selling it. I got the painters in and they did the whole place in cream. That'll be fine for the time being.'

'If you need any help…'

'Thanks, but no. The sitting room and bedroom are both sorted, and the kitchen and bathroom aren't my choice of colour but they're both pretty much new. I have all that I need.'

He nodded and followed her through into the kitchen, still looking around as if he was assessing the house to see if it was fit for purpose. Callie ignored him, fetching a vase from under the sink and dumping the flowers into it.

'Coffee?'

He shook his head. 'I've had too much coffee already this morning. Do you have tea?'

'About twenty different kinds. My mother's been bombarding me with tea for months.' She opened the cupboard to reveal the stack of boxes.

'Regular tea will be fine, thanks. Your mother… She knows about this clearly.'

'Yes, she and Paul have been great…' Callie bit her tongue. She deserved the look of reproach in Ben's eyes. Other people had known about this for months when he hadn't.

'Paul's her partner. They've been seeing each other since last year and… I think she's found someone at last…' Callie saw her hand shake as she reached for the teabags.

'I'm glad you have their support.' His face softened suddenly. 'You have mine too.'

He carried the tea into the sitting room, and Callie let him do it. If he wanted to help, he could do the things that didn't matter so much, the things that she wouldn't miss if he left. Then he produced a piece of paper from his pocket.

'I've written this down. What I'd like…' He handed the paper to her and Callie took it, unfolding the single sheet. There were just two sentences and numbering them seemed a little over the top.

'Number one… No. I don't need you to help support me and my baby.'

'*Our* baby,' he corrected her quietly.

He could say that when his ankles started to swell and he couldn't get comfortable in bed at night. When tying his shoelaces started to become an exercise in balance and reach, and he'd been prodded and pummelled by what seemed like a whole army of doctors and nurses. Callie let that point go in favour of the greater principle.

'My photography's going well and… I'm sure I can manage.' *Sure* was a little bit of an overstatement, *hope* was a bit more like it. But she'd explored her options and the photographs she'd taken at the fire station had added a different slant to her portfolio, which had helped a lot.

'My offer isn't negotiable.'

'Neither is my refusal.'

They'd fallen at the first fence. Quiet words, which showed how diametrically they were opposed in their approach to this. Callie stared at him and he stared back.

Ben was the first to break the impasse. 'Okay. I'll set up an account and pay the money into it monthly. If you need it, it's there. If not, it's there to cover her university tuition fees.'

'She's going to university?' Callie hadn't thought that far ahead. That was the difference between them, she was focussed on getting through the next few months and he didn't have to worry about that. He could afford a few big dreams.

'When she's eighteen she can do whatever she wants. The money will be there for her.'

'Okay. I...guess that's between you and her.' If it happened then it happened. If Ben lost interest, she could provide for her daughter.

'We're in agreement, then?'

'Yes.'

'And number two?' He was doing it gently, but he was pushing her.

'Yes. You can have regular access to her, that's not a problem. We can sort something out...'

'Can we do that now?'

'No. We have to see what works and...' She

felt dizzy, and Ben was going too fast. Sudden pain shot across her belly.

'Callie…? Are you all right?'

'Yes!' She took a breath to steady herself. 'Yes, I'm fine. I dare say something's hit a nerve somewhere…' If this was a new pain, to add to the other nagging aches and pains, it was one that Callie could do without. Particularly when she was engaged in negotiating with Ben over her daughter's future.

She shifted on the sofa, feeling a sudden warmth between her legs. Before she could check to see what it was, Ben's face told her that something really *was* the matter.

CHAPTER FOURTEEN

HE'D EXPECTED HER to agree to number one straight away, and then fight him on number two. It was just like Callie to do the opposite. She might look a little softer but she was still determined to do things her way.

And determined not to take his help. Her face had contorted in pain, but she'd just kept on insisting that she was all right and it was just one of those things.

Then she'd moved, and he'd seen the blood soaking into the pale fabric of the sofa cushions. That definitely wasn't one of those things, and she wasn't all right.

She knew it too. She looked at him with frightened eyes, perhaps realising that even her carefully primed defences couldn't stop this.

But she was still trying to deal with it alone. Callie tried to get to her feet, her hand reaching for her phone, and he gently sat her back down again. 'Stay still, Callie. I'm calling for an ambulance.'

'Yes.' There was no compliance in her eyes but there *was* fear. He'd take fear. Whatever allowed him to help her. Ben took his own phone from his pocket, dialling quickly.

'Tell them... I don't think I'm in labour yet. I feel light-headed and sick, and...' She looked miserably at the spreading stain on the sofa. 'Severe vaginal bleeding... Possibility of *placenta abruptio*.'

Ben relayed the information, adding that Callie was a paramedic to justify the attempt at self-diagnosis. The woman on the other end of the line told him that someone would be there in ten minutes, and Ben begged her to ask them to hurry. He wasn't exactly sure what *placenta abruptio* was, but he knew enough to understand that it wasn't good.

'I'm just going to breathe and stay calm.' Callie took the words right out of his mouth. 'They'll be here soon.'

'That's exactly right. Do you want to lie down?'

'Yes... I think so.'

He gently helped her to lie down on the sofa. Then knelt down beside her and held out his hand.

'Go on. Take it. We can forget it ever happened.'

She quirked her lips downwards, and then she took his hand. 'Our secret, eh?'

'Yes. Our secret.'

For a moment the old understanding flashed between them. If Callie would accept this temporary truce, that was a beginning. Temporary could be stretched until it resembled permanent.

'I need to call my mum.' She gestured towards her phone again. Ben picked it up and switched it on, scrolling through the contacts and dialling the number before giving it to her.

It seemed almost wrong to listen to her conversation, but Ben wasn't going to leave her side. Callie was making an effort to downplay the situation, but when she handed the phone over to him so he could take her mother's number, the woman on the other end of the line sounded worried.

'Text me when you know which hospital they're taking her to. And don't you leave her alone for one second until I arrive.'

'I won't.' He wasn't even sure whether Callie's mother knew who he was, and she rang off before he could tell her. He should have let her know that he would do anything, if only Callie and the baby were all right.

He held her tightly when her face contorted with pain and didn't let go when it passed. Ben was used to waiting for medical help, he'd done it many times before, but this time… It had never felt that he was so inextricably linked with someone that his own survival was entirely dependent on theirs.

'They're here…' Blue flashing lights reflected through the windows and across the room. Ben hurried to the front door, wishing that the two men would walk a little faster up the front path.

He ushered them through to the sitting room and the older of the two knelt beside Callie. Their exchanged smiles made it clear that this was one of Callie's colleagues.

'All right, lass. Symptoms…'

Callie rattled her symptoms off, seeming to rally a little now that the ambulance was here. Someone she knew. And trusted. Ben stood back, out of the way, fighting the urge to be the one that she clung to.

'I think there's a possibility of *placenta*—'

'Give it a rest, Callie. I can't abide patients who tell me what's wrong with them, you know that.'

'So what do *you* think?'

'Possibility of *placenta abruptio*.' The paramedic gave her a reassuring smile. 'We'll get you to the hospital now, and they'll confirm it.'

Callie puffed out a sigh. 'That's a hospital stay at best. Or they may have to do a Caesarean…'

'We'll see. One thing at a time, eh? You know the doctors don't much like it when we tell them what to do, even if we do know better than them.'

'Tell me about it.'

Ben was at a loss. He couldn't walk away and leave the medics to do their job, the way he usually did. He had to *know*. 'Please…what's wrong with her?'

The man flipped a querying look at Callie and she nodded. He turned to Ben. 'It's possible that Callie is suffering from *placenta abruptio*, which is where the placenta separates from the wall of the uterus. It's something we take very seriously.'

'What does that mean?'

'It means that I might have to have the baby by Caesarean section. Now, before it becomes distressed or I bleed to death.' Callie was obviously in no mood to beat about the bush.

'Right. Thanks. We'll go now?'

'Yes, my partner's gone to get a wheelchair. We'll get her there as quickly as we can.'

'I'd like to go with her.' The desperate feeling that he had no right to insist on anything, but every reason to, gripped Ben.

The paramedic's gaze flipped once more to Callie in an unspoken question and Ben held his breath.

'Let him come. He's the father.'

* * *

Callie was surrounded by nurses and a doctor as soon as she reached the hospital. The ambulance crew stayed for ten minutes before they had to leave for another call, leaving Ben standing alone in the corner of the cubicle.

'She'll be all right. She's in good hands.' A nurse patted his arm. She was obviously the one who'd been assigned to calm the nervous father.

'Thank you.' Ben craned his neck, trying to hear and see as much as he could of what was going on. If there were decisions to be made, he at least wanted to know what they were, even if it was unlikely that Callie would give him any say in them.

Finally, the doctor turned and explained to him that Callie was bleeding heavily and that a Caesarean section was needed. He added that it was a straightforward procedure and that Ben could look forward to welcoming his baby a little earlier than he'd thought.

Ben nodded his thanks, omitting to say that he hadn't had a chance to think anything yet. The doctor hurried out of the cubicle, and finally Ben could take his place at Callie's side.

'Hey, there.'

'You're still here?' She looked up at him a little blearily.

'No, I'm just a figment of your imagination.'

'Okay. That's fair enough.' She smiled at him, squeezing his hand, and Ben felt his overworked heart in danger of bursting.

A nurse arrived to take Callie down to the operating theatre, and hard on her heels came a woman who bore a marked physical resemblance to Callie.

'Mum…' Callie called for her, holding out her hand, and Ben stepped back again, wondering what he was supposed to do now.

There was no chance to do anything. The nurse released the brakes on the trolley that Callie was lying on, and before Ben could tell her any of the things he wanted to say, the trolley was manoeuvred out of the cubicle. Callie's mother ran a few steps to catch up, taking Callie's hand as she was wheeled away.

He should be glad that her mother had arrived in time. Callie had clearly arranged that her mother should be there at the birth, and she needed her right now. But all Ben could see was that Callie was being taken from him.

A neatly dressed man of about sixty approached him. 'You're Ben?'

Ben nodded, keeping his eyes on the trolley and the retreating figures of the nurse and Callie's mother.

'I'm Paul. Callie's mother's partner. Shall we wait together?'

* * *

Ben followed Paul to the waiting room in a daze, glad that at least someone seemed to know what to do next. Stopping to drop a few coins in the vending machine, Paul brought two cups of tea over and sat down next to Ben.

'The waiting's the worst part. It'll all be worth it, though.'

'You have children?' Ben took a sip of his tea, thankful that this kindly man was here. Without someone to talk to he'd probably be banging his head against the wall.

'Two girls. My wife died when they were teen-agers.'

'So you brought them up on your own?'

Paul nodded. 'I didn't think I'd find anyone else. But then I met Kate, Callie's mother. Just goes to show…'

'Goes to show what?'

'That you never know what's around the corner, waiting for you.'

Ben allowed himself a smile. Callie had said that her mother had finally found the right man, and he was willing to grab at any slender proof that life might allow second chances. He had to believe that was the case, that Callie and their daughter would be all right, and that somehow they could find a way through this.

* * *

After what seemed an age, a nurse popped her head around the door of the waiting room, calling out Ben's name. He stared at her for a moment, almost afraid to hear what she'd come to tell him.

'Go on. What are you waiting for?' Paul spoke quietly.

Ben got to his feet and hurried over. The nurse smiled at him.

'Mother and baby are both doing well. Callie's had a Caesarean section, and she'll be very drowsy for a little while. Her mother's with her and they'll be taking her back to the maternity ward soon. You can go and see her there.'

'Thank you. And the baby?'

'It's a beautiful, healthy girl. She's a little premature, so she'll be looked after in the high dependency care unit for a few days, but that's just a precaution.'

'Can we see her?' Ben heard Paul's voice behind him. 'I'm sure Ben would like to see his daughter.'

'Yes. Very much.' He was feeling a little unsteady on his feet, but he shot a grateful look in Paul's direction.

'I'll take you there now.' The nurse began to walk briskly along the corridor, leaving Ben and Paul to follow.

The high dependency unit was a large, quiet ward, all gleaming surfaces and technology. The nurse guided Ben to an incubator, and he looked at the tiny baby inside, willing her to open her eyes.

'She doesn't need any help breathing, and she's a good weight for being a month premature. Six pounds exactly.'

Ben couldn't stop staring at his daughter. *His* daughter.

'Kate said that you were going to call her Emily.' The nurse spoke again.

'Emily?' Ben could feel tears forming in his eyes.

The nurse laughed quietly. The fact that Ben didn't even know his daughter's name didn't seem to bother her. Maybe all new fathers were this dumbfounded, or maybe she'd just seen everything. 'I'll leave you here to get acquainted.'

'May I take a picture?' Something to take away with him, to remind him that this was real.

'Yes, of course. Callie got to hold Emily for a little while in the recovery room, but I'm sure she'd like a photograph.'

Ben took his phone from his pocket. At last, there was something he *could* do.

Paul accompanied him back to the maternity ward and they waited outside Callie's room for a moment before Kate appeared, her face shining.

'I won't stay, she's still groggy. But she'd like to see you for a couple of minutes, Ben.'

'Thank you.' Ben wondered whether the suggestion had come from Kate or from Callie, but right now that didn't matter. He had his entry pass and he wasn't going to argue.

'I think we should be going. We can come back in the morning.' Paul put his arm around Kate. 'We'll see you then?'

Wild horses wouldn't keep him away. He shook Paul's hand, thanking him, and opened the door to Callie's room quietly. She was lying still on the bed but her eyes were open, following him as he moved towards her. He smiled and suddenly a broad grin lit up her tired face.

'You did it, then.'

'Yes. I did it.'

Their connection, which had seemed so remote over the last two days, seemed forged anew. Ben sat down beside the bed.

'And you made a great job of it. She's beautiful.'

Callie chuckled quietly. 'Yes, she is. She's got blue eyes…'

'Most newborn Caucasian babies have blue eyes.' It was one of the few things that Ben knew about babies. He was committed to knowing more as soon as he possibly could.

'She has a little bit of dark hair as well.'

Like her daddy. The thought made the world swim around Ben slightly. He wondered whether Callie would ever say them.

'I didn't see her hair, she had one of those little hats on.'

'She has a tiny birthmark on one of her fingers and she weighs six pounds. That's good for a late pre-term baby.' Tears formed in her eyes. 'I know I'll be able to see her in the morning but I just want to hold her now.'

'Of course you do…' There was no point in saying that this was for the best, and that their baby was being well looked after. Callie already knew that.

He reached into his pocket and brought out his phone. 'Here…' He'd taken a video of the tiny baby, keeping it running until the memory on his phone gave out. Holding it in front of Callie, he saw her immediately transfixed by the small screen, her face mirroring each movement and each of the tiny grimaces on her daughter's face.

'She knows how to pull a face already.' He reached for Callie's hand, squeezing it, and she squeezed back. The regulator on the transfusion lead attached to her arm dripped a little faster.

Tears formed in Callie's eyes. 'Yes, she does. Thank you, Ben. Thank you so much.'

'Keep watching. And keep squeezing my hand.'

She glanced at the regulator and nodded, then her gaze was fixed back on the small screen. When the tiny baby sneezed, her own face scrunched up, as if she was trying not to.

'How are you feeling?'

'Very numb still.' She tried for a laugh and then thought better of it. 'The bits of me that aren't numb are starting to hurt.'

'You'll feel better soon.' Ben had no idea whether or not that was correct, but it sounded like the right thing to say. 'You're strong. Like her.' *That* he knew.

'Play it again.' She nodded towards his phone.

'Okay.' Ben wanted to watch it again, too. 'Keep squeezing my hand.'

The nurse brought in a milky drink for her, and Callie took one taste and scrunched her face up. Ben laughingly encouraged her to drink, helping her hold the cup. She was weak and shaky still, and if she was going to be able to hold her baby, she needed to build up her strength.

She was fighting sleep, wanting to see the video a third time, but Ben switched it off and made her close her eyes. As they talked quietly, Callie's voice became slower, more slurred, and finally she drifted off to sleep.

Ben settled in the easy chair, watching her. He imagined Callie wouldn't like the idea of his standing guard over her while she slept, but since she *was* asleep, she didn't have much say in the matter.

He was beginning to relax, soothed by the sounds of Callie's regular breathing, when the door opened quietly and a dark-haired nurse entered. She smiled at Ben and walked over to Callie's bedside, reaching out to brush her forehead with her fingertips.

'I'm Sophie, Callie's friend. You must be Ben.' She spoke in a whisper.

Ben nodded. When Callie's family and friends were around, his claim to her seemed to grow more tenuous. If Sophie wanted to throw him out, she probably had the authority to do so.

'How is she?'

'The doctor said she's doing well. She's very tired…'

'Yeah, I'll bet she is. I came as soon as my shift ended.' Sophie sat down in an upright chair next to the bedside. 'How are you?'

'Me?' Ben wondered how much Sophie knew.

She grinned at him. 'I was in the car outside your apartment yesterday, waiting for Callie. She left it a bit too long before she told you so this must all be a shock.'

The impulse to defend Callie tightened in his chest. 'It's okay. She had her reasons.'

'All the same…' Sophie subjected him to a steady, enquiring look, and when Ben didn't reply, she let the matter drop. 'You've seen your daughter?'

'Yes. She's beautiful… Perfect.'

Sophie looked at him thoughtfully. 'You want to stay?'

Ben had nowhere else to go. The only home he had was with Callie and his little girl. And whatever Callie had told her friend about him, it couldn't be all that bad, because she seemed willing to let him remain here.

'Yes. I…' He shrugged. 'If the staff tell me to leave, I'll sit outside.'

'Okay, I'll have a word. They won't kick you out.' Sophie rose, stopping for one last look at her friend. 'I'll see you again?'

'Yes, you will. Quite a lot, I imagine.'

'Good.'

When the door closed quietly behind Sophie and Ben had settled back in his chair, it occurred to him that he'd passed some kind of test. There would be more to come, a lot more, but at least this was a start.

CHAPTER FIFTEEN

BEN HAD BEEN there for her. He'd done more than possibly could have been expected of him over the last few days, coming to the hospital every morning and spending the day there. The joy and indignity of being a new mother had made Callie forget for a while that she'd promised herself that she could do this on her own.

When he'd told her that he was taking two weeks' emergency leave from work, she'd protested. But he hadn't listened, insisting that he wanted to be there. He clearly wasn't sleeping much and even though he smiled every time he looked at their little girl, there were dark rings under his eyes.

Callie watched him as he sat rocking their baby. She'd be released from the high dependency unit in a few days, and then Callie could take her home.

'I've been thinking. About her name.' Callie

hadn't once called her daughter Emily, it didn't seem to suit her.

'Yeah?' Ben had steered clear of the decision-making. He was there, always listening, but he always deferred to Callie's opinion.

'Do you think that she really looks like an Emily?'

Ben considered the thought carefully. 'Most of the babies here don't really *look* like their given names. I dare say they'll grow into them.'

That was about as close as Ben was going to get to speaking his mind. Callie pursed her lips. 'Only… I just can't get used to Emily. I love the name, but…it just doesn't seem to fit.'

Ben chuckled. He obviously thought the same. 'So what did you have in mind?'

'I don't know really.' Callie had thought of a few names she liked better, but she wanted to hear what Ben thought as well. 'Any ideas?'

He smiled and shook his head, answering too quickly to have thought about it at all. 'No, not really.'

'Go on. Don't you have any favourite names?'

Ben sat for a moment, holding the tiny baby. Then he drew in a breath. 'What about Riley? You probably don't like it…'

Callie said the name a couple of times, trying it out for size. She liked it a lot. 'What made you come up with that?' Perhaps one of the guys at the fire station had a kid named Riley.

'When my sister was pregnant, she wanted my brother-in-law to come up with a few names...he was a bit stuck and we went to the pub to brainstorm it. I liked Riley but he didn't, so it never made it onto the shortlist. It means *valiant*.'

That was exactly what Callie was going to teach her daughter to be. Valiant. 'I really like it.'

Ben looked shocked. 'Do you?'

'Yes, I do.' She cooed the name a couple of times, and the little girl opened her eyes. 'She likes it too...'

'She's probably just hungry.'

Callie ignored him. She knew what her daughter liked and didn't like. 'I think Riley's a great name. Let's call her that.'

He gave her a smile so bright and enchanting that there was no question about Ben's approval. And no question that he appreciated having been asked in the first place. 'If that's what you want, I think it really suits her.'

Callie had brought Riley home when she was five days old. Her mother had moved in for a while to help with the baby and Ben had visited every day, busying himself with helping to unpack crates and finding jobs to do around the house when he hadn't been spending time with his daughter.

It had been time well spent. He and Callie had talked about access to Riley on an ongoing basis, and it seemed she was committed to making it easy for him and working around his shift patterns. And he'd fallen in love with his daughter.

All the same, the idea of going back to work was a relief. Helping make Callie's house into a home had been a little too much like having someone to build a home and family with. They were lost dreams, and he needed to get back to the realities.

But even the reality of going back to work had changed. When he walked into the ready room he found that Blue Watch had embraced the unexpected news that he was a father. A loud bang produced a shower of sparks and streamers and everyone crowded around to shake his hand.

Ben endured the jokes and friendly advice and managed to ignore the words 'dark horse' when he heard them. Eve had waited until he was alone again and proffered a brightly wrapped package that she'd been holding behind her back.

'Eve...thank you.' Ben didn't know what to say. This was an aspect of parenthood that he hadn't quite counted on.

'It's just a little something…for the baby.' Eve seemed as embarrassed as he was.

'I…' Ben stared at the package. 'Should I open it now?'

'No, boss! You're supposed to give it to Callie and let her open it.' Eve grinned suddenly. 'You haven't got the hang of this yet, have you?'

'No, I haven't. It was all a bit of a shock.' Ben wondered whether Eve would ask. He almost wished that she would. 'I didn't expect anyone to make a fuss…'

Eve shrugged. 'A baby's something special. It doesn't matter how it happens.'

All the same, Ben felt like a fraud. His only real contribution to Callie's pregnancy had been the obvious one at the very start. And now people were slapping him on the back and giving him presents.

'I don't know… How do you do this, Eve?' He'd take whatever advice was on offer.

'Babies don't come with an operations manual—you have to deal with everything as it comes. You'll be fine.' Eve shot him a smile and turned away.

He retreated to his office, making a mental list of all the things he needed to do now that he was back at work. Then his phone vibrated. Callie had sent a video of Riley. Ben stared at the notification, his finger hovering over the play icon. Then he threw his phone down onto the desk, hearing the bell ring as he did so.

The crew had been summoned to a small fire on one of the few pieces of waste ground left in the densely populated city. It was a simple enough job to extinguish the flames but it seemed somehow surreal.

'Steady on, boss…' Ben almost tripped over a coiled length of hose and he turned just in time to see Jamie flash a knowing smile towards Eve. Yeah, okay. He still had his baby head on.

And Callie hadn't exactly helped. He'd managed to get his head around not seeing her and Riley for five days, but now all he could think about was that video.

'Sorry…' Ben decided that if he couldn't watch where he was putting his feet the best place for him was out of the way, standing next to the tender. He was used to the fact that Blue Watch could operate perfectly well without him, he'd encouraged that during their training exercises. Being a liability was new, though.

This couldn't go on. Compartmentalisation was the way forward. When he was on duty he had to be a leader. Off duty was the time to be a father. Ben decided not to look at his phone again until the shift was finished.

* * *

That evening, when he retrieved his phone from his locker, there was another text from Callie. Before he had a chance to look at it, the phone buzzed again.

How was your day?

Callie was probably feeling the same as him, that all this was unbearably strange. They both had to find their feet, but it was just as well to start as they meant to go on.

Good. Can't text while working.

He sent the text before he had time to think that it sounded a little curt. His phone buzzed again, almost immediately.

Sorry.

Ben cursed under his breath. He'd upset her now.

It's okay. Busy day.

It hadn't been a particularly busy day. If he was starting as he meant to go on, a little honesty would be better than excuses. But the text had been sent now. He typed another.

Thanks for the video. Looking forward to seeing you on Wednesday. Eve sent a present. I'll bring it with me.

His phone buzzed again. It would actually be easier to call Callie but something stopped him.

That's so kind. What is it?

So Callie didn't know that they were supposed to open it together either. Ben smiled. They were both on a learning curve.

I don't know. She says you have to open it. Wait until Wednesday.

He added a smiley face and put his phone in his pocket, slamming his locker door shut. Wednesday seemed a long time away, and he'd just ruled out any possibility of more texts in the meantime. That was how it should be, though. They were both adults, and surviving for a few days on their own shouldn't be that hard.

CHAPTER SIXTEEN

IT HAD BEEN five days since she'd seen Ben, and Callie had spent much of that time thinking about him. Perhaps it was her hormones.

The texts had been a mistake. Ben had made it very clear that he didn't want to indulge in the to and fro of sending videos and *How are you?* messages on the days he was working. And Callie had decided that she needed to clear the air, leave nothing unspoken, because it was the things that were left unsaid that generally did the most damage to a relationship.

He was on her doorstep at exactly two o'clock on Wednesday afternoon. Ben was nothing if not prompt.

'How are you?' That was always his first question, and always accompanied by a tight smile.

'Fine, thanks.' Callie stood back from the door to allow him in. As he passed her in the hallway she caught a delicious curl of his scent. She needed to ignore that. He was Riley's father, and that was bound to flip a switch somewhere.

'Where's Kate?' He walked into the sitting room, looking around.

'She's popped out for some shopping. Riley's sleeping.' Maybe he wouldn't notice that this opportunity to talk had been carefully contrived.

If he did, he gave no hint of it. Ben's smile was inscrutable, calculated not to give anything away. Inscrutable was probably a lot easier for him than it was for her at the moment as he didn't have raging hormones to contend with.

'I wanted to say...' Callie lowered herself carefully onto the sofa. 'I'm sorry about the texts.'

He shook his head. 'It doesn't matter. That was a great video of Riley.'

It *had* mattered. Callie had known it almost as soon as she'd sent it, and when he hadn't replied straight away it had confirmed her fears.

'Ben, I wish that...'

'What?' He gave her an innocent look.

'I wish that we could have an adult conversation. There are things that we need to work out and... Can't you just tell me how you feel about this?'

'I don't matter. You and Riley are the ones who matter.'

'Stop it. You *do* matter.' Callie could feel tears in her eyes and she blinked them away impatiently. 'Look, there's no walking-away option here. Not for me anyway. Riley will always be my daughter and you'll always be her father.'

He looked at her thoughtfully. 'I don't have a walking-away option either.'

'Right, then. In that case we both need to say how we feel. Because that's the only way forward.'

'You're right.'

Callie puffed out an exasperated breath. Ben had been letting her off the hook about things, telling her that everything was okay for the last three weeks. He couldn't keep this up and at some point he was going to explode.

If he couldn't do it now, maybe he'd think about it and do it later. Callie wondered whether she should get up and make a cup of tea, and decided that the effort of standing could wait a little longer.

'I'm angry.' His quiet words didn't sound all that angry but at least he'd said them. It was a start.

'About?' Callie felt herself starting to tremble.

Ben sucked in a deep breath. 'Were you really so afraid of me that it took eight months to work up the courage to tell me you were pregnant?'

'I'm not afraid of you. After what you went through with Isabel, I decided to wait until…you could be sure.'

'I imagine it had been obvious for a while.' He shook his head, clearly trying to understand but unable to. 'Isn't it just that you wanted to be the one to provide for Riley? You didn't want me to have any part in her life?'

The quiet vehemence in his tone shocked Callie. But this was what she'd wanted, to clear the air between them and for Ben to tell her how he felt.

'Yes, I want to be able to provide for Riley on my own. There's nothing wrong with that, is there? But you had a right to know, and you have a right to be able to see her as well. You're her father.' The sudden thought that Ben might have been questioning that struck Callie. 'You can take a test if you're in any doubt...'

His face softened suddenly. 'I'm in no doubt. I trust you, Callie, but I just wish you'd trusted *me* a bit more.'

'I tried. I sent you a text but you didn't reply.' Now she thought about it, not replying to uncomfortable texts was Ben's modus operandi. She should have taken that into consideration.

'It was one text.' He spread his hands in disbelief. 'You said you wanted to meet for lunch, not that you were pregnant.'

'Because it would have been such a good idea to tell you that I was pregnant by text, is that what you're saying?'

They fell silent, staring at each other. Callie was the first to give in. 'Look I know I did this badly but I did the best I could at the time. I'd hoped that we'd have a bit more time to get used to this but… I failed there as well, I couldn't even make the full term of my pregnancy…'

The nurses had told her that it was common for women who'd undergone emergency deliveries to feel a sense of failure. She'd said the very same thing to women herself when she'd attended emergency calls. Callie hadn't realised just how all-consuming and corrosive the feeling was until now.

Ben shook his head, running his hand through his hair in a gesture of frustration. 'That's not a failure, Callie. But not telling me…it made *me* fail. I wasn't there for you during your pregnancy and now…it's a lot to get my head around in such a short time. I'm struggling and I need some…distance.'

Callie's mouth felt suddenly dry. Failure. Distance. It hadn't taken Ben long to change his mind and now he was backing away.

'What kind of distance?'

'I just need to compartmentalise a little. When I'm at work I need to concentrate on that. When I'm here I can concentrate on you and Riley.'

That didn't sound so bad. One box for Ben's job and another for her and Riley. Callie could live inside that box for Riley's sake. She'd even decorate.

'That's okay. I can live with that.'

'Really?' He looked almost surprised.

'Yes. I need some time to myself too and… that sounds like a good arrangement.'

Her head approved of it at least. Her heart and her hormones wanted to know where he was at any given point in the day and wanted Ben here when he wasn't at work. But her head was her best and strongest ally.

The sound of a key in the front door made them both jump. Ben smiled a hello as Callie's mother walked past, towards the kitchen, and then he got to his feet. 'I should go…'

'No, Ben. You're not going anywhere.'

'Your mum's here and I don't want to argue.' His face was impassive again. Closed off.

'Fair enough. But you're here to see Riley and I don't want her to be one of those kids who gets caught up in her parents' problems. Whatever happens between the two of us shouldn't ever affect your time with her.'

He nodded. 'You're a great mother, Callie.'

The compliment made her want to burst into tears. Not now. Not when they seemed to be making progress.

'Then be a good father and go and fetch her. I dare say that Mum's making a cup of tea.'

Ben had smiled a lot since Riley had been born, but none of his smiles had had the carefree warmth about them that Callie had seen in his face last Christmas. But this one… He was getting there. A weight had obviously been lifted from his shoulders.

They were making progress. Maybe not quite in the direction that Callie had imagined, but that was what compromise was all about.

CHAPTER SEVENTEEN

AGAINST ALL ODDS, they were making it work. Ben wondered if that would be the one thing that he looked back on as the crowning achievement of his life.

They were doing it for Riley. She meant more than his anger and Callie's independent streak. More than their confusion and the feeling that neither of them were a match for the situation. And he told himself that Riley meant more than the tenderness that he saw in Callie's eyes from time to time, and which echoed in his own empty heart.

As late summer gave way to autumn and then winter, they were turning their uneasy truce into a way of life. Callie started to organise afternoon photography shoots, starting with portraits and visits to the hospital to talk about the possibility of using her portraiture as therapy. She always worked on Ben's days off, and after some weeks of having Kate there to help him look after Riley while Callie was gone, he took the plunge and cared for his baby daughter alone.

The times that Ben had come to treasure were when Callie wasn't working. When all three of them could spend time together. The everyday things that had meant so little to him took on a touch of magic. Going shopping for food or for a walk in the park. Watching as Riley began to notice that there was a world around her, and seeing her discover it.

'I have to pop in to the hospital before we drop Riley off with my mum. There are some notes I need to pick up from Dr Lawrence in preparation for this evening.'

'You're sure your mum's happy to look after Riley this evening?' Callie was working, taking photographs with a man who was recovering from severe burns.

'She's always happy to look after Riley. I don't know what time I'll finish, and you're working tomorrow.'

'You're going to be great.' He could see that Callie was nervous. He'd felt much the same when he'd gone back to work after Riley was born, and he'd had far less reason. This new project, in partnership with the burns unit at the hospital, had taken a lot of work and planning.

'Thanks. I just hope… I just want to do this right.'

Callie gave him an apprehensive smile. This was one of the times when he wanted to fold her in his arms and tell her that he believed in her. But Ben couldn't, because hugs were for Riley. If he and Callie happened to touch during that process, it was an electric pleasure that he never allowed himself to think about.

'Trust me. You'll do it better than right.' Ben shook off the temptation that was pounding in his veins and lifted Riley out of her baby bouncer.

Watching him trying to bundle Riley into her snowsuit seemed to take Callie's mind off her own self-doubt for a moment. Ben heard a stifled giggle behind him as the little girl managed to pull her left arm back out of the sleeve for the third time.

'I think she must get this from you,' Ben joked, finally managing to get both Riley's arms into the snowsuit at the same time and pulling the zipper up.

'And I thought that she'd inherited her unco-operative streak from her father.' Callie laughed and Riley started to wave her arms, joining in. That was one thing that the little girl definitely got from her mother. Her smile, and the way that it made Ben's heart turn to mush.

Ben concentrated on his daughter, leaving his feelings for Callie out of the equation. 'Do you want to walk to the hospital or take the car?'

'Shall we walk?'

'Yes. I could do with stretching my legs.' His arms and legs still ached a little from his efforts at a factory fire two days ago. But that wasn't for Callie to know.

As they drew near the hospital gates she seemed more buoyant, talking about her work and the new opportunities and challenges it would bring. That was Callie all over—the closer at hand the challenge, the better she rose to it. It was good to hear her so excited now. Maybe in time he'd share some of the challenges that his work brought…

No. Keeping that separate worked for both of them. Ben didn't function well at work when he was thinking about Callie. They'd been through that already.

In front of them a car wove across the road. Ben instinctively put his arm out, pushing Callie and the pram behind him, although the car wasn't going at any great speed. It drifted to a halt halfway across the pavement, pointing towards the entrance to the hospital.

He felt Callie start forward and he pulled her back, gripping her arm tightly. 'Stay here with Riley. I'll go and see…'

She looked as if she was about to protest and then she nodded. Ben ran towards the car, seeing a man slumped across the steering wheel as he neared it.

He tried the door and it was locked. But the front window was slightly open, as if the car's occupant had been in need of some air. He forced it down, reaching in to switch off the engine and open the driver's door.

'He hasn't crashed, the airbag hasn't even been activated,' Ben called back to Callie, knowing somehow that she'd wouldn't have stayed right where he'd left her. She couldn't help coming a little closer.

'Maybe taken ill at the wheel.' Callie's voice was even closer than he'd expected and when he looked around she was craning to look inside the car, one hand on the pram.

'Callie, will you—?'

'Stay back? No.'

Ben gave in to the inevitable. Callie was better qualified to do this anyway. He took hold of the pram while she knelt down beside the car, examining the man quickly.

'Looks as if he's had a heart attack. Maybe he felt unwell and tried to drive himself to the hospital.' She looked up at Ben. 'Get my phone, will you? It's tucked in the side of the pram.'

Ben felt for the phone and found it. Callie grabbed it from him and made a call, speaking quickly. Then she put the phone back into her pocket.

'They're sending someone down straight away.' She unzipped the man's jacket, pressing her head to his chest, her fingers searching for a pulse. 'We can't wait. He's in cardiac arrest.'

'We need to get him out of the car?' If they were going to attempt resuscitation, they couldn't do it while the man was still in the driver's seat.

'Yes.' Callie pre-empted Ben's next thought and stood back. 'You can lift him better than I can.'

Ben knew that the scar from the Caesarean still pulled a little sometimes, and reaching into the car meant she'd have to lift and pull at the same time. He let her take charge of the pram, thankful that she hadn't ignored her better judgement. Carefully he manoeuvred the man out of the car, laying him down on the pavement, and Callie slipped a baby blanket under his head.

'Should I start resuscitation?' He wasn't going to allow Callie to do that either. Ben had enough training to do the job.

'Yes. You want me to count?'

'Yep.' Ben felt her eyes on him as he positioned his hands on the man's chest in the way he'd been taught. Callie started to count and he followed the rhythm that she set for him.

'Keep going, you're doing great. They're coming…' He heard Callie give an impatient huff. 'Stay back, will you? There's nothing to see here. Let the paramedics through.'

Ben smiled grimly, briefly aware that the small crowd that had formed behind them on the pavement had suddenly begun to disperse. There was the sound of voices and then a man knelt down beside him.

'Swap on three.' Callie counted the beats and Ben sat back on his heels, letting the paramedic take over. An ambulance was approaching the gates and its crew were unloading a trolley, ready to take the man into the hospital.

He stood up, retreating to where Callie stood with the pram. She smiled up at him and Ben felt her hand slip into his.

'Good job, Ben.'

'Great counting.' He smiled down at her. 'I'm impressed by the standing back, too.'

'Don't push it.' He felt her elbow in his ribs and a sudden tingle ran down his spine.

Riley's first medical emergency. She'd come through it with flying colours, dozing in her pram the whole time. He and Callie had come through it too, relying on each other and working as a team. It had stirred an ache in Ben's chest. Memories of when they'd been more to each other than just Riley's mum and Riley's dad.

Callie reappeared from her meeting with Dr Lawrence, a manila envelope in her hand. It was only a short walk to Kate's house, and once they'd handed Riley over to her grandmother there was no reason for him to stay. He'd pick up his car keys from Callie's and go home.

As they walked up her front path, Callie's phone rang. She answered it, cradling the phone between her ear and her shoulder as she opened the front door and motioned him inside, listening intently to someone at the other end of the line.

'No… No, Eric, that's absolutely fine. We'll do this when you're ready, not before… It's no inconvenience. It's really important that you take whatever time you need.' She was smiling into the phone. 'Give me a call tomorrow when you're feeling better. If you want to talk about things a bit more, I can always drop in and see you…'

A few more reassurances and then Callie finished the call. As she met Ben's enquiring gaze, the smile faded from her face.

'What's up?'

'The guy I was going to take photographs with this evening just cancelled. He's had a bad day and doing things when he isn't ready is just going to be counterproductive.' Callie shrugged. 'That's okay. He still wants to do it, just not this evening.'

She was clearly disappointed. Callie had prepared for this so carefully and now that it wasn't going to happen she seemed at a loss as to what to do next. Ben made for the kitchen. 'I'll make you a cup of tea before I go.'

There was no excuse to keep Ben there now but Callie suddenly didn't want him to go. That was a sure sign that she should send him on his way as soon as politely possible.

'It's good that he felt able to phone and cancel.' She sat on the sofa, her coat and gloves next to her on the cushions. 'I suppose I'd better go and get Riley.'

Ben put two mugs of tea down on the coffee table. 'Drink your tea first. There's no rush. Kate's got a full programme of baby activities planned, and she won't much like it if you turn up on the doorstep before she's had a chance to try Riley out with the baby learning centre.'

Callie chuckled. 'True. Mum's determined that she's going to be a genius.'

'I'll settle for her being able to do whatever she wants.'

'Yes, me too.' That was one thing that she and Ben could agree on without any danger of their shared ambitions starting to look like a relationship.

'I know you've done a lot of preparation for

this evening. You must be disappointed.' He leaned back on the sofa cushions, sipping his tea.

This crossed the boundaries that she and Ben had set for themselves. But maybe she needed him to put a toe across those lines at the moment.

'I just feel…' She shook her head, trying to work out exactly how she did feel. 'I'm rather hoping I haven't lost my edge. That man this afternoon…'

'Lost your edge? Seriously? From where I was standing, it looked as if you were in charge the whole time.'

It was nice of him to say so. She'd stood by, counting helplessly, clinging to the pram, while he'd done all the real work. 'I'd have had him out of the car and started resuscitation without even thinking about it once upon a time.'

'And you'll do it again, but not before you're fully fit.' He held up his hand as she protested. 'I know you feel as if you are, but these things always take a bit longer than you think. You were exactly where you needed to be, and where Riley needed you to be.'

What would she have done if Ben hadn't been there, though? Callie dismissed the thought. He wasn't the only person who could have helped, even if, at the time, it had felt that he was the only person she needed in the world.

'Do you want to stay and watch a film with

me?' She could allow herself that at least. 'Then I'll go and pick Riley up.'

It was a departure from their usual way of doing things, and he took a moment to think about it. Then he nodded. 'I'd like that. Why don't you choose something and I'll go and get us some snacks from the kitchen?'

CHAPTER EIGHTEEN

CALLIE'S IDEA OF snacks while watching a film usually extended to opening a packet of crisps. She flipped through the list of films, trying not to smile. It wasn't exactly unexpected that the man with the best-stocked fridge she'd ever seen had found the packet of popcorn at the back of the cupboard, and from the sound of it was putting it to use.

She still hadn't settled on a film when he appeared in the doorway of the sitting room, holding a bowl of popcorn in one hand and a large platter in the other.

'What's this?' She moved her coat so that he could sit down beside her.

'Just popcorn. And I raided your chocolate stash and found some bits and pieces in the fridge...'

To good effect. A thick, melted chocolate goo was in a small bowl in the centre of the platter, surrounded by an assortment of fruit, chopped and arranged carefully. Callie grinned at him.

'When it's time to teach Riley to cook, will you promise to do it?'

Ben chuckled. 'Taste it before you say that.'

He reached forward, taking half a strawberry from the pile and dipping it into the chocolate. When he held it to her lips the warm and cold sweetness, coupled with the scent of having him close, made her forget about everything else.

'Mmm… That's…very good.' Too good. Callie could feel heat rising to her cheeks, and she covered her confusion by reaching for the TV remote. They could draw back now and nothing would be lost. It would just be a moment that meant nothing.

'Have you chosen a film?' If Ben had felt anything then he too seemed unwilling to acknowledge it.

'How about this?' The first one on the list looked as good as any other, and when Ben nodded she pressed the start button. They'd watch the film and then she'd collect Riley and Ben would be on his way.

This was strong magic. The wish to take Callie's mind off her disappointment had turned into the sudden feeling that kissing her was the absolute next thing to do. If that was just an illusion, it was a hard spell to break.

He held out as long as he could. But Callie seemed about as interested in the vivid special effects on the TV screen as he was. All he could see was her.

'Carrots? Really?' They'd worked their way through the fruit on the platter now.

'I used whatever I could find…'

'So this is an experiment?' She dipped the baton into the chocolate and tried it. 'It's….different.'

Ben couldn't move. He didn't have the strength to resist when she dipped the rest of carrot into the fondue and held it to his lips. And by some sorcery he thought he tasted only Callie.

He should stop before he was completely beguiled. But the look in her eyes kept him motionless. And then the touch of her finger on the side of his mouth, wiping away a smear of chocolate, turned his blood to fire.

He could kiss her now, and then they could forget all about it and go back to what they'd been for the last three months. What had worked. *Yeah. Tell yourself that…* Ben ignored the voice of warning echoing softly in the back of his head.

She dipped one finger into the chocolate and put it into her mouth. And he was lost. When he reached for her, Callie was there, melting into his arms as if there had never been any other place she'd wanted to be.

Her body was different now, but it hadn't forgotten what it was like to feel Ben close. However had she thought it could?

She felt Ben's hands spreading across her back. Just the way they had before...

Not *just*. It was more. All they'd been through since last Christmas, all the hurdles they'd managed to overcome lent a depth and an exquisite tenderness to his kiss. A slow burn, which couldn't be quenched.

He was holding her away from him a little, but seemed helpless to stop her when she moved closer, feeling his body hard and trembling against hers. Callie kissed him again or maybe Ben kissed her. They were so connected, so much at one with each other, that it was impossible to tell.

'I've missed you so much, Callie. But...'

Did there always have to be a *but*? Always some reason why they couldn't do what they both wanted to do? Callie couldn't bear to pull away from him. If he was going to reject her, he'd have to do it while she was still in his arms.

'But what?'

In the heat of his sudden smile nothing could

hurt her. 'You couldn't be any more beautiful to me than you are now, Callie. But you've just had a baby and…to be honest, I don't even know the right questions to ask.'

It was all right. Everything was all right again. Callie put her finger over his lips and shifted onto his lap. Face to face, staring into his eyes.

'You want to ask whether I'm ready. And how far we can go together.'

Ben chuckled softly. 'I knew I could count on you to come to my rescue. I don't suppose you have the answer, as well as the question?'

'My answer is that I feel ready, and I trust you to be with me and take each moment as it comes.' She kissed him, a new warmth flooding her body. She was safe with Ben, he'd never hurt her. And he'd never hurt Riley.

'I'm following your lead. One word from you and we stop. I'm trusting you to say that word.'

'Do I get to say "Come upstairs" as well? "Let me take your clothes off"?' she teased him.

'Yeah. You can say that as soon as you like.'

Their lovemaking hadn't been so physically active this time around. But Ben's tenderness had been deeper and wilder than before. He'd told her all the things she wanted to hear, that she was beautiful and that he desired her. And the connection was stronger than ever as he watched for her every reaction.

She wanted to stay curled up in his arms but the evening had slipped away in a slow burn of delight and it was getting late.

'I should go and fetch Riley.' She nudged at his shoulder.

'I can go if you want to stay here.' He opened his eyes sleepily.

'No, I'll do it. Mum's expecting me.'

Ben nodded. Maybe he too wanted to keep this between the two of them. Callie wasn't ready to make it a part of her everyday life, not just yet.

His gaze followed her as she got out of bed. Picking up her clothes from the floor, she instinctively held them across her stomach, hiding the scar and the stretch marks.

'Don't cover them up.' His murmured words made her stop. 'Or am I going to have to take a photograph to convince you?'

Callie dropped her clothes back onto the floor.

He grinned, blinking his eyes as he imitated the sound of a camera shutter. 'That's the picture I want...'

Ben refused to think about the complications. This felt right. Getting out of bed, he threw his clothes on and went downstairs. The sitting-room light was still on and he cleared away the scattered remains of the popcorn and fondue. Still wrapped in the satiated warmth of their lovemaking, he sat down on the sofa and began to doze.

He didn't hear Callie coming back. When he felt tiny fingers on his face, his eyes snapped open in alarm and he heard Callie's laughing admonition.

'Don't punch Daddy in the face, sweetie.'

Two different pieces of his life crashed together headlong. He rubbed his eyes, trying to make sense of the gorgeous chaos.

'Sorry.' Callie was sitting on the edge of the sofa, one hand on Riley's back to steady her. 'Did we startle you?'

'I must have dozed off.'

And woken to find that the simple, comforting rules that he'd built his life around didn't hold true. He could follow the pattern he'd used to keep his work and his private life separate, and put his relationship with Callie and his relationship with his daughter into two separate boxes all he liked. Keeping them there was an entirely different prospect.

But somehow it didn't matter. He reached for Riley, picking her up for a hug. It seemed suddenly possible to hold everything that he most loved in the world in his arms. When Callie moved closer, nestling against him, that possibility became a reality that took his breath away.

'This...is nice.' Callie looked up at him as he put his arm around her shoulders. 'Different...'

He kissed Callie's cheek and then bent to kiss the top of Riley's head. 'You want to take a moment to get familiar with it? I'd like to.'

She laughed suddenly, and Riley imitated the sound in her own sing-song way. 'Yes. I could definitely get used to this.'

Riley was crying. And then the bed heaved as Ben got out of it and she heard the sound of him pulling on his jeans.

'I'll go...'

Callie muttered an acknowledgement. This moment ranked with all the others that she wanted to keep. She could hear Ben singing quietly, and when she opened her eyes she saw his silhouette, rocking their baby in his arms.

'I'll take her downstairs. You get some sleep.'

She heard Ben chuckle. 'You'll do no such thing.'

The bed moved again as he sat down on it, and Callie wriggled over towards him, still wrapped in the duvet. All the love in the world seemed to reside within the circle of his arms.

Love? Was this what this was? Or was it just two people thrown together who wanted to make a family from the materials to hand? At the moment the future seemed like a distant ogre that could be fought later.

'I'll have to go soon.' Ben's voice rang with regret and Callie glanced at the clock beside the bed. It was an hour's drive home and then he had to get to the fire station to start his shift.

'How long?'

'Not yet. Half an hour.'

He seemed to want that half-hour to last as much as she did. Riley quietened suddenly in his arms, as if she too knew that this was something special.

'When will I see you again?' The question she'd been determined not to ask came naturally suddenly.

'Maybe we can…spend the day together when I'm next off shift?'

Five days. Probably six, to give him the chance to sleep after his night's work. It seemed like an age but Ben was probably right. This was too fragile a thing, too precious, and they should go slowly.

'Yes, I'd like that. Give me a call then?'

She felt him move and his lips brushed her forehead. 'Yeah. I'll give you a call.'

CHAPTER NINETEEN

NO THOUGHT WENT into it. Ben's training kicked in as soon as he realised he was falling, and he bent his knees, landing on his feet and then rolling.

The pain came soon enough. He couldn't stand so he crawled, dragging his useless leg behind him. There was only one aim in his head. Get out. If he wanted to hold Callie and Riley in his arms again, he had to get out…

Blind, dogged effort gave way to relief when he felt himself being lifted and carried the final few yards out of the building. Eve's voice penetrated the haze of pain. 'Stand down, boss. We've got you.'

He realised that he'd been fighting, still trying to get to his feet even though he was well clear of the building now and he could see the sky. Hands found the place where his ribs hurt most and he groaned…

Sirens. The ambulance was running on a siren and it was making his head hurt. Why couldn't they just turn it off? He managed to pull the oxygen mask from his face, getting out just one word before the ambulance paramedic gently put it back in place.

'Callie...'

Callie ran from the hospital car park, making straight for the ambulance crews' entrance into A and E. She hadn't heard from Ben since he'd left her early yesterday morning, and she hadn't expected to. When Eve had called, it had felt like a physical blow.

As luck would have it, her mother had been there, and she'd been able to leave Riley with her. The roads had been clear and she'd made the drive to the hospital in just over half an hour.

An ambulance had drawn up and the crew was wheeling a gurney through the automatic doors into A and E. She recognised Ben's shock of dark hair and put on a final sprint for the doors before they swished closed again, feeling the scar across the base of her stomach pull a little as she ran.

'Callie Walsh. I'm a paramedic...' She fumbled in her bag, showing her ID to the ambulance driver, who was standing next to the gurney. 'I'm...with him.'

Luckily *with him* was a good enough explanation. Callie wasn't sure how else to describe herself.

'Okay. We're finding a doctor now....' The driver nodded towards his partner, who was navigating through the melee of people, all of whom seemed to have something to do.

'How is he?' Callie could see dressings on Ben's arm and an immobiliser on one of his legs. An oxygen mask obscured his face and his eyes were closed.

'He's breathing on his own, no critical injuries that we can see. His arm's burned and his leg's broken.' The man allowed himself a tight smile. 'I'm glad you're here.'

Before Callie could ask why, Ben stirred. He seemed to be trying to reach for something, and she caught his flailing hand, telling him to stay still. At the sound of her voice he opened his eyes suddenly.

'Callie...?'

'Everything's all right, Ben. You're at the hospital and you're safe.'

He seemed to only half comprehend what she was saying but half was enough. Ben's fingers tightened around hers and the urgency of his movements subsided.

'What happened?' Callie murmured the question to the ambulance driver.

'A floor gave way and he fell from the first to the ground floor. He crawled a fair way before the crew could get to him and bring him out.'

And Ben was still on autopilot. That steely determination of his hadn't quite worked out that he was safe yet.

'He's been like this all the way here?'

'Yeah, he's been drifting in and out. When he was awake he was thrashing around, calling for you. And Riley…?'

'That's our daughter.'

'Right.' The ambulance driver looked round, seeing his partner approach with a young doctor. 'Here we go…'

Callie followed as the doctor shepherded them into a cubicle with the gurney. She could hardly breathe. Ben hadn't called out for his work family, the team he'd come to rely on. He'd wanted her and Riley.

It was nothing, an automatic reaction. She'd heard patients call out for all kinds of people. The doctor introduced himself as Michael, and Callie flashed her paramedic's ID again, when it looked as if the next thing he would do was to tell her to stand back.

The doctor thought for a moment. 'We're very busy and it's not as if I couldn't do with your help.'

Could she keep her tears under control and think like a medic? Right now she'd do whatever it took. 'I won't get emotional.'

Michael nodded. 'Okay. I want you to step

back if that changes, Callie. We all have our limits, and I can deal with whatever needs to be done.'

Barely. It would be quicker and better with two. But Callie nodded her head. 'I understand.'

'In that case, I want you to try and keep him conscious and focussed.'

Michael was giving her a task that involved as little medical intervention as possible. That didn't matter, as long as she could be close to Ben. And it would be a lot easier for the doctors and nurses if he could react to their questions, rather than alternating between a semi-conscious state and trying to fight them.

As Michael turned his attention to the nurse who had just arrived with a burns trolley, Callie surreptitiously reached for the penlight on the counter. Keeping him conscious wasn't so very different from checking for a concussion.

She tapped his cheek with her finger. 'Ben... I've got you now, and you're safe. Look at me...'

He opened his eyes. Clear blue, in stark contrast with the grime streaking his face. They held all the need that she'd seen when he'd cried out for her in the night, but this time he needed her in a different way, one that was a lot harder to respond to. He was hurt, and it was up to Callie to pull him back from a precipice that she hadn't dared think about.

Callie swallowed hard. She knew her job, even if she knew nothing else at the moment. She just had to do her job.

'Do you know where you are, Ben?'

His lips formed one word. 'Hospital…'

'Great. That's right.' Callie caught his free hand in hers. 'I want you to squeeze my hand if you feel any sudden pain.'

He nodded, his gaze fixed on hers. When she shone the penlight, his pupils reacted correctly to the light and Ben appeared to know what was going on around him. More than that. His gaze seemed to know everything, the way it always had…

Tears threatened, and Callie made an effort to stop thinking that way. If she showed any signs of distress, Michael would have to make her stand back.

'What's the date today?' She covered her confusion with a question, moving the face mask a little and leaning in to hear the answer.

'First of December. The monarch is Queen Elizabeth. My name's Benjamin David Matthews and my daughter's name is Riley.' Ben caught his breath in pain. 'She has the cutest smile.'

Okay. She got it. Ben had been through this procedure before and he knew all the answers to the questions.

'Your middle name's David, is it?' She forced

a smile. In all the hundreds of little details about their lives that they'd exchanged, middle names had never come up.

'Yes.'

'Just stay still for a moment…' Callie let his hand drop and felt him clutch at her blouse. Fair enough. How many other patients had reached for her, holding on as if that was all that was keeping them safe. She carefully examined him for any cuts or bumps on his head, finding nothing.

'Your leg and your arm hurt…' She could see from his eyes that they did. 'Anything else?'

She was caught again in his gaze. 'Nothing… hurts.'

Nothing had been able to hurt her either when she'd been in his arms. 'Ben, cut the macho act. What else?'

His eyelids fluttered down in a sign of acquiescence. 'My side…'

Callie turned, and saw that Michael had uncovered a large, rapidly forming bruise on his ribs. It could be a sign of a cracked rib or even internal bleeding. He was probing it with his fingers and Ben groaned, his hand clutching tighter onto her shirt.

'I want you to breathe in…' Michael caught his attention and Ben's gaze turned to him. But however hard she tried, Callie couldn't get him to loosen his grip on her.

As Callie had anticipated, the break was a bad one, and his leg was going to need surgery. The doctor thought that they could get Ben down to the operating theatre straight away, and left Callie with him to wait for news.

He was slowly coming around. Warm, and about as comfortable as pain killing drugs and pillows could make him, Ben began to loosen his grip on her shirt. Then he let go.

'It won't be long now.' Callie had gone to speak to one of the nurses to find out what was happening.

'I'm sorry, Callie.'

'Be quiet. You have nothing to apologise for.' Callie heard a tense edge to her voice. Ben must know as well as she did that her greatest fear was that the father of her child wouldn't come back one day, and that it was agony to see how close he'd been to that possibility today.

'You should go… Riley…'

'Riley's fine, she's with Mum. You're the one I'm worried about.' She bit her lip as tears sprang to her eyes. Callie had resolved not to mention the word 'worry'.

He reached for her hand, squeezing it tightly. 'I'll be okay…'

She wanted to raise his fingers to her lips, but she couldn't. Instead, she laid her hand lightly on his forehead. It was a gesture of comfort that didn't seem too dangerous at the moment.

'I'll be here when you come out of surgery. I called Eve to let her know how you were doing and she said that some of the crew would be coming down here later as well.

'No fuss, Callie…'

'You're not the boss here, Ben. You'll do as you're told and we'll make as much fuss as we want to. You're in no position to stop us.'

He frowned, clearly searching for an argument. Then Ben's lips quirked into a smile. 'Yes, ma'am.'

'That's better.'

When she was alone she could cry. She could think about the ramifications of seeing the father of her child injured in the line of duty. How it felt more awful than she could ever have thought it would. But for now she had to be strong.

Yesterday afternoon and evening was a blur. The only thing that had been in really sharp focus was Callie. Ben had woken up in his hospital bed this morning, and as Eve had promised him before she left last night, he was hurting in places he hadn't even known he had.

Ben submitted to all the doctors' and nurses'

requests of him, but his mind was elsewhere. His injuries had changed everything between him and Callie. She'd done everything to reassure him, but he had seen through the façade. He'd made a reality out of her worst fears.

When visiting time came, he couldn't help but watch for her, almost hoping that she'd decided not to come. But she did, and when she walked through the doors of the ward, carrying Riley in a sling, his heart took over from his head and beat wildly.

He couldn't take his eyes off her. As she sat down next to his bed, she smiled at him. 'How are you today?'

'Much better, thanks. What about you?' Callie looked tired. As if she hadn't had a wink of sleep last night.

'I'm fine.' The hint of protest in her voice told Ben that she very definitely wasn't fine. He reached for her hand, feeling it cold in his.

'No, you're not.' He flashed her a *Don't argue* look, and she quirked the corners of her mouth down. 'I know that this isn't where you ever wanted to be.'

He'd put her here, though. He'd made love to her, and now she was sitting by his hospital bed. The different strands of his life had become tangled and knotted and it was time to unravel them.

'I don't know what you mean.' She bent down,

reaching into the bag she'd brought with her, but she couldn't disguise the flush in her cheeks.

The worries that had been swirling in his head consolidated into certainty. Callie would make an effort to ignore her fears, but she couldn't overcome them. She might stay with him because of love, or from a misplaced sense that it would be better for Riley. She might stay to nurse him back to fitness. Whatever the reason, she'd get to the point where concerns over his safety made her feel threatened and unsafe, the way she had when she'd been a child, and that would break them apart. There could only be one thing worse than never having the family he wanted, and that was having them and then losing them.

'We have to talk about this, Callie.'

She puffed out a breath, one hand moving protectively to the back of Riley's head. The little girl was curled against her chest, fast asleep.

'Okay. It's difficult, Ben, is that what you want to hear? I'm dealing with it.'

No. She wasn't. The only way forward was to rely on what he knew worked. Compartmentalisation.

'Callie, neither of us can deal with this, we both need to back away. What happened between us the other night can't happen again. We can't take that risk.'

She caught her breath. He could see the question in her eyes. *Don't you care?* If she didn't know that he cared for her, she didn't know anything about him, but Ben couldn't say it. Callie could ask him anything, but that was the one question he wouldn't answer.

'We can't take the risk with Riley, you mean?' Eventually she settled on an easier question.

'No, we can't. We promised that our relationship wouldn't ever hurt her, and a week ago that promise was easy to keep. I think we should make sure it stays that way.'

'But…we already…' She looked around at the other beds, as if to check that no one was taking an interest in their conversation. 'We've already spent the night together and things were fine… They weren't just fine, they were great.'

'And now they're not. After one night we can go back and pick up our lives. After six months or a year… I couldn't make it back from that.'

'But what if we *can* make it work?' She was frowning, her face haggard with lack of sleep. Callie was so intent on just getting through this, but he could see in her eyes that she was fighting a losing battle with herself.

'Can you honestly tell me that this is what you want for Riley? Having her mother worry like this every single day? Because it's not what I want for her and it isn't what I want for you and me either.'

'I…' Callie's protest died on her lips. 'No. It's not what I want.'

'So let's make things easy, shall we? Go home. I'll give you a call in a couple of days when I'm out of here. We'll work from there.'

Her back stiffened suddenly. 'I can't do that. You need someone to look after you, Ben.'

That was the least of his worries right now. He reached for his phone, switching it on and showing her the texts. 'What I *need* is an appointments system.'

She flipped through the texts, a tear rolling suddenly down her cheek. 'I guess the fire service looks after its own.'

'Yes, we do.' Ben had always thought of his crew as family. Now they seemed a shadowy second-best to the one he was sending away. The one that couldn't ever be.

'Okay.' She began to unclip Riley's sling, running her finger across the little girl's cheek to wake her. Then she held her closer to the bed so that Ben could reach her. 'I want you to kiss your daughter, Ben. Tell her you'll see her very soon.'

'So how's Ben?'

It was a natural enough question. When Callie had accepted an invitation to lunch at Eve's, she'd expected she would ask and had her answer ready.

'I haven't seen him for two weeks. My mum and her partner have been taking Riley over to see him. We decided that it's best for all of us if we just stick to our access arrangements.'

'That's what he said when I saw him last. I just wondered what your side of the story was.' Eve flashed Callie an apologetic smile.

Even in the quiet agony of their parting it seemed that she and Ben were maintaining a united front. Callie hugged Riley tight. She was the one thing that made any sense in any of this.

'It is what it is. He's a great father to Riley, and that's what matters.'

'Yep. I can't imagine Ben would be anything else.' The oven timer sounded from the kitchen and Eve got to her feet. 'That's our lunch…'

Thankfully, there were no more questions about Ben. But Callie was learning that not talking about him didn't stop her from thinking about him. All roads seemed to lead back to him at the moment.

'Doesn't your husband worry? About your job?' Eve had been talking about how they managed Isaac's care when she was on shift, and Callie couldn't help asking the question that was pounding in her head.

'Yes, he worries. I worry about him as well.' Eve grinned in response to Callie's questioning look. 'He's a civil servant. Desk jobs can be tough, too.'

'Not as tough as your job surely?'

'I don't know about that. He's not as fit as I am, and he doesn't get to work off the stress. I'm a bit concerned about his cholesterol.'

'What level is he?' Callie asked automatically, and then thought better of it. 'Sorry. Professional interest.'

'That's okay. He's at five point five.'

'That's not so bad. It could be lower, particularly at his age, but a bit less saturated fat in his diet and some exercise should bring it down.'

'I'm sending him to the gym.' Eve grinned. 'I reckon that I might as well get the benefit of this health kick of his, and I'm looking forward to a little finely toned musculature.'

Callie almost choked on her food. Ben did finely toned musculature well. Very well. Thinking about it wasn't going to help.

'So it's not really an issue for you, then?'

'Yes, of course it's an issue. But I was a firefighter when I met Danny, and we both knew what we were signing up for when we got married.' Eve shot Callie a knowing glance. 'And I'm not Ben.'

'Is there a difference?'

'Ben's a leader. He's responsible for everyone, and he's the one who makes the hard decisions.

Do you know why it was him who fell through that floor the other day and not his partner?'

'No. Why?' Callie almost didn't *want* to know.

'Because Ben goes first. He always does. He never asks any of us to do anything that he won't do, and he never gives up. That's not an easy thing to live with.'

Callie could feel the flush spreading across her cheeks. Ben was a true hero. That *was* hard to live with, but she couldn't be more proud of him.

'If you see him…'

'I'm dropping in tomorrow. The guys are great at going round there and ordering in a pizza, but Ben's probably worked his way through most of the fresh food I left him last time. You want a status report?'

'Yes… Yes, please. But please don't tell him.' The least that Callie could do was to watch over Ben from afar. It couldn't hurt if he never knew about it.

'I won't. I'll call you tomorrow evening.'

CHAPTER TWENTY

Christmas Eve

BEN WAS SPRAWLED on the sofa, looking miserably at the Christmas tree. It was still bare, looking like something that had wandered in and settled itself by the hearth but had no real place there.

He'd had such hopes for this Christmas. This year, Blue Watch had Christmas Eve off, and he'd been planning to see both Callie and Riley. The day would be full of sparkle, all the pretty things that Riley loved. After their night together, he'd briefly hoped that he and Callie would be able to share some magic of their own, too. It would be the best day of the year.

Instead, it was shaping up to be the worst. Ben shifted uncomfortably on the sofa, the cast on his leg cumbersome. His leg throbbed and the burns on his arm were still painful.

The buzzer sounded and Ben laboriously made his way over to the intercom. That was one of the disadvantages of a large, open-plan living area. Everything was so far away.

Whoever it was didn't buzz again. They must know that he was slow at the moment. Perhaps it was one of his crew, coming to try and cheer him up. He'd done his best when Eve had popped round the other day with her little boy, but when she'd left he'd felt even more upset and alone.

'Ben. Are you there?' Despite the crackle of the intercom, he recognised Callie's voice.

'I'm here.' His hand hovered over the door release and then dropped to his side. He'd made his decision about seeing Callie, and he wasn't going to change it just because he was at a low ebb.

'Are you going to let me in?'

'No. Go home, Callie.'

'I've just come from home. It's taken me an hour to get through the traffic…' Her voice rang with dismay. 'I have Riley with me, and she's freezing cold. And she's crying.'

Ben couldn't hear any crying. But Callie obviously wasn't going away and he couldn't leave her on the doorstep. Despite himself, Ben felt a little thrill of excitement as he pressed the button to release the main door.

'Thank you!' He heard Callie's final words before the intercom cut out. They were laced with frustration and he could just imagine her rolling her eyes.

It would be a few minutes before she got herself and Riley into the lift and back out again. Ben used the time to stack that morning's breakfast things into the sink and dump the newspapers that littered the sofa onto the coffee table in something that resembled a tidy pile. It was the best he could do to make it look as if he was managing for himself.

He'd barely got settled, back onto the sofa, when the door drifted open and Callie appeared. She was carrying Riley in a body sling over her red coat, a richly patterned skirt grazing the tops of her fleece-lined boots and a large bag over her shoulder. Riley was dressed in green, with a little elf hat on her head. When Callie pointed towards Ben, Riley stretched one arm out and began to chuckle.

Ben hardly dared move. He watched as Callie kicked the door closed behind her and walked towards him. A short struggle with the body sling and then she put Riley down on the sofa next to him. 'Look, Riley, there's Daddy.'

Riley reached for him, and Ben lifted her onto his lap. He hugged his little girl tight, kissing her.

'She doesn't look as if she's been crying.' He decided to call Callie's bluff.

'She cheered up when she saw you.'

From the little jut of her chin it seemed that Callie found Riley's sudden change in mood just as unlikely as he did. She shrugged, looking around the apartment.

'Nice tree. You've decided to go for the minimalist look this year?'

'The guys brought it round but they had to get to work and I haven't got around to decorating it yet. Sorry about the mess, I wasn't expecting company.'

'That's all right. I can tidy up a bit...' Callie seemed intent on finding something to do.

Enough. He couldn't bear this. 'Callie, why are you here?'

'I knew you'd be disappointed about not seeing Riley, and Mum's busy. I brought some shopping as well. Eve said you were running out of a few things...'

'*Eve* said?'

'You know I speak to Eve.' She flushed, putting her bag onto the kitchen counter and starting to empty it.

He knew it. Callie and Eve had struck up a friendship, and had seen each other regularly since Riley had been born. It had been hard, in the last three weeks, not to ask Eve how Callie was and clearly Callie had been similarly tempted.

'Callie, you didn't need to come all this way to restock my cupboards. And it's great to see

Riley, but that could have waited until Kate was free to bring her.'

She froze, staring down at the groceries that she'd taken out of her bag. 'Yes. You're right.'

'So what *are* you doing here?'

Callie felt her cheeks burn. This was the biggest risk she'd ever taken in a life dedicated to avoiding risk.

She swallowed hard. If he was going to send her away, she might as well say what she'd come to say first.

'I've made a decision, Ben. I couldn't do anything about it when I lost my father or my home, but I can do something about losing you. You said to me once that there are some things that are important enough to take risks to achieve, and without that a life can become meaningless...'

Callie stopped for breath. Ben was staring at her, and Riley was suddenly still in his lap. The little girl was looking intently at her too, knowing maybe that this was a moment that could change their lives.

'Go on, Callie.' At least he was going to hear her out. That was something.

'Eve told me that you were injured because you always go in first. You never ask anyone to do anything you won't do.'

Annoyance flashed across his face. 'That's not quite how it is.'

'Don't try to protect me, Ben, that's exactly how it is. And you're exactly the kind of man that I want in Riley's life. Someone who isn't afraid to lead and who'll be there for her whatever happens.'

He nodded. 'I *will* be there for her.'

Callie took a deep breath. Now or never... 'You're exactly the kind of man I want in *my* life, too.'

'Callie, we've been through this already—'

'Yes, we have. But I was wrong to let you go. All I could think about was that I might lose you, but... I never thought that the only person who could make me happy enough to deal with my fears was you.'

He shook his head. She'd messed up all over again. Callie began to panic, as the consequences of the risk she'd taken began to swell in her heart.

'Say something, Ben. If you want me to go...'

Suddenly he smiled. 'Stay here, Callie. With me.'

She could feel heat spreading from her cheeks to her ears and then around the back of her neck. She'd taken the first step, and Ben had responded with another one. She wanted to fling herself into his arms, but it was all too soon for that. If he just let her stay for a little while, she could show him that she wasn't going to pressure him any more.

'Right, then. So you'll tell me where the decorations are?'

Ben nodded towards the door that led to the other side of the apartment. 'There's a big cupboard. Through there…'

She hadn't been through there since last Christmas. Then it had seemed a concrete reminder for Ben of all the things he hadn't believed in any more. Now maybe it was a reason for hope.

'I'll…go and get them, shall I?' She was still standing yards away from him, in the kitchen area, but Callie couldn't shake the feeling that they were closer now than they'd ever been.

'That sounds great. We can decorate the tree together.'

That sounded wonderful. Callie almost ran towards the door, twisting the key feverishly in the lock, before Ben changed his mind.

It seemed that Callie couldn't sit still. Ben knew exactly how she felt, but it was a little more difficult for him to give in to the temptation to quiet the pounding of his heart with physical activity.

Callie had changed everything. The tearful grin she'd given him had made him realise why his life had been so dark recently. Without her,

Christmas was just another drab winter day. But she'd turned it into a time of hope.

In a whirl of energy she fetched the decorations and examined the contents of his fridge, while the coffee machine dribbled the last of his fresh coffee into two cups. Then she declared the food situation to be worse than she'd imagined and decided they should go out, because he couldn't possibly go without turkey sandwiches at Christmas time.

'It's too late. We'll never get a turkey on Christmas Eve.'

'It's early still and when I drove down the High Street the shops were heaving. Look at Ebenezer Scrooge—he managed to find a turkey on Christmas morning.'

Ben chuckled. 'As I remember, he sent a boy to find the turkey. And that was a long time ago. Things have probably changed.'

'Yes, they've changed. We have supermarkets now. Do you have a sock that I can put over your cast to keep your foot warm?'

Ben gave up. It was hard enough to resist Callie when she wasn't around, and now it was downright impossible.

'Upstairs. I'm afraid it's a bit of a mess…'

Callie chuckled. 'I'll survive. Running up and down the stairs to tidy up isn't exactly a priority when you're on crutches.'

'I'll have you know that my physiotherapist was very impressed with my grasp of stair climbing techniques. She may even have mentioned the word *perfect*...' He called after her.

Ben could hear the sounds of pillows being plumped and the duvet being rearranged. 'Don't bother with that. Socks are in the top drawer of the dresser.'

'Okay...' It sounded as if Callie was ignoring him because she was still walking around, probably picking up the clothes he'd left on the floor. 'We'll go shopping and then we'll decorate the tree.'

Callie knew that she was pushing things further than she'd meant to go. But Ben was smiling, that luminous blue-eyed smile that she remembered from last Christmas. The moment he stopped, she'd take a step back, but she couldn't while it was still on his face.

Ben's car was bigger than hers and he could get into the passenger seat more easily. Callie manoeuvred the SUV into a parking space as close to the supermarket entrance as she could. It went without saying that leaving him in the car with Riley while she got the shopping was too much time apart. And even if everything did take a little longer, Ben made good use of the opportunity, dropping things they didn't need into the trolley and making faces at Riley.

'I can hear carol singers.' He was looking around as Callie loaded the boot of the car, trying to work out from which direction the voices were coming.

'Perhaps we can drive past...'

'Can't we take a walk over?' They must be at the Market Square on the High Street.

'How far is it? Can you make it?'

He nodded. 'This is Riley's first Christmas. I'll make it.'

Riley had seen carol singers already, but Callie decided not to take away the magic. This was the first time she'd see them with her father. She flipped the remote to lock the car doors and put Riley into the body sling, feeling her daughter's hands to make sure that she wasn't too cold. The little girl was as warm as toast and as cute as a button in her green elf hat.

The carol singers were obviously an established choir and they had a band with them. The music swelled as they got closer, and the crowd around them let Ben through when they saw his crutches. Callie stood close. Even if he couldn't hold Riley, he could at least touch her.

She began to hum along with the carols, and Riley followed her example, tuneless and wavering, not pausing when the singers finished and the band turned the pages of their music sheets. Ben's smile made Callie's heart quiver.

Maybe it was just Riley who made him smile. But Ben slipped the crutch out from under his left arm, putting it with the other one under his right. Callie felt his arm curl lightly around her waist, a little tighter when she nestled against him. She'd missed this so much, his scent and the taut strength of his body. It had seemed like an impossible dream that he would hold her again, and that Riley should be with them in a circle of warmth between her mother and father.

But they couldn't stay long. Ben began to shiver, from the cold and the effort of standing like this, and when Callie led him away, he didn't protest. It had been a few precious minutes, but whatever the future held for them, that could never be taken away.

CHAPTER TWENTY-ONE

IT WAS ALL his Christmases rolled into one. Callie had decorated the Christmas tree, and Ben had helped as best he could. Riley had wanted to touch all the decorations, and he'd carefully held them in front of her, allowing her to play with the felt ones he'd bought for her.

'*Ew...* This one's all slimy.' Riley had handed Callie a fabric star, pointing at the tree. She was getting the hang of this quickly. 'She's been sucking it, hasn't she?'

'Yes, I think she's hungry.'

'I'll make up a bottle.' Callie grinned at him and headed for the kitchen.

'Don't bother with that, I'll make myself scarce. She's already had one bottle today.' However much he wanted to recreate the feeling he'd had watching Callie feed Riley at the hospital, he shouldn't rush things. If Callie wanted this space, he had to respect it.

'Don't you want to feed her?'

'Yes, but…' He realised suddenly that it wasn't space that Callie wanted. She'd suggested a bottle so that he could feed Riley. Warmth rushed through his veins and he nodded.

'Well, then.'

Callie prepared a bottle and put Riley into his arms. The little girl tugged at his shirt, pressing herself against him. This was the best time in the week. Along with all the other best times that he had with Riley.

He glanced up at Callie, and suddenly the world tipped and he slid helplessly into her smile. *She* was watching *him*.

Riley had fallen asleep, and Callie reckoned she'd have at least an hour before she woke up again. She knew that Ben wouldn't do this in front of his daughter.

'Let me see your arm.'

'No need. It's okay.' Apparently he wasn't intending to do it in front of Callie either. But if Riley clearly had her father wrapped around her little finger, Callie had a few more weapons in her arsenal. Being able to form words was a start.

'When did you last have it dressed?'

'A few days ago. It'll be all right until after Christmas.'

'I'm sure it will be, but *I* want to take a look. The health visitor left some sterile dressings?'

Ben grinned. 'In the cupboard, over there. You treat all your patients like this?'

'Not all of them. The firefighters are generally the worst, they're a pretty stroppy crowd. I keep my special tactics for them.'

'Special tactics?' He chuckled, and Callie fought to keep a straight face.

'You don't want special tactics. You're not up to it at the moment.'

'No, I don't think I am.' He undid the zip of the warm sweater he was wearing and slipped it from his shoulder, rolling up his sleeve.

Callie carefully peeled off the tape that secured the dressing pad, making sure that nothing was stuck to the wound. The burn looked better than she remembered it, but it was still red and painful.

'And the health visitor's happy with your progress?'

'I don't much care what the health visitor thinks. Since you've decided to take a look, I'd like to know what *you* think.'

Callie stared at his arm. She wasn't accustomed to being fazed by any degree of injury, a paramedic who was wouldn't be of much use. But this healing burn had turned her stomach to jelly.

'I think…you're doing well. If it keeps healing like this there won't be any scar. How's your leg feeling?'

'It feels…like a broken leg. It'll heal.'

'And I don't need to make a fuss?' She grinned up at him, and saw laughter reflected in his eyes.

'Consider it your sole prerogative to make as much fuss as you like.'

Callie re-dressed the burn as gently as possible. Ben didn't make a sound, although she knew it must still hurt.

'How does that feel? Not too tight?'

'No, it feels fine.'

She pulled his sleeve back down again carefully. As she reached to help him back into his sweater, she felt his fingers on the side of her face, tipping it up to meet his gaze. All the tenderness that she'd missed so much.

'Thank you, Callie.'

She felt her fingers turn clumsy. Liquid fire was running through her veins, not burning but warming her after what seemed like a very long winter.

'How's your side? Since it's my prerogative to make a fuss.'

'Still a bit painful. They said that this kind of bruising would take a little while to heal.'

Callie nodded. 'It is healing, though?'

He nodded, pulling the side of his shirt up a little, and Callie carefully pulled it a little farther. The bruise that had covered most of his left side was blotchy and beginning to disperse. Callie felt a tear run down her cheek and turned her face downwards so he wouldn't see it.

'Hey. What's this?' His fingers brushed her face again, and this time they were trembling. 'Please, Callie. Don't cry, I'm not going anywhere. Riley's going to have to put up with me for a good while longer. So are you, for that matter.'

'Of course we are.' Callie wiped her face with her sleeve. 'I think I just needed to look and… I needed to face what happened to you. I never really did, not at the hospital, I was too afraid of breaking down.'

'And now you have faced it?' Ben's voice was tender.

'I can leave it behind.' She sat down next to him on the sofa, feeling his arm curl around her shoulders. She already had more than she could have hoped for, but she was greedy. Callie wanted one more thing.

'I was going to take Riley over to Mum's tomorrow morning for lunch with her and Paul. She asked me if you'd like to come.'

'She…did?' He raised his eyebrows in disbelief.

'Well… Actually, she said it was a shame that you were alone this Christmas, and she wished you could be with us. If she knew I was here, she would have told me to ask you to come.'

'You're sure about that?'

'Yes, positive. You'll be more than welcome, Ben. And it's Riley's first Christmas. If you'd like to come, I can pick you up in the morning.'

He was silent for a moment. Callie felt her heart thump in her chest.

'I'd love to come. But you can't make a two-hour round trip on Christmas morning.'

'It's okay. The roads will be clear.' Perhaps she shouldn't push it.

'You could, but if you'd like to stay here to-night, you and Riley can take the spare room.'

'I suppose…that might be more convenient.' The pounding of her heart seemed to be block-ing her throat.

'Let's do that, then. Thank you.'

Ben's head felt as if it was about to explode. Was it really possible that so much could change in the course of just a few hours?

When she'd looked at his injuries, she'd cried. She'd let herself feel something, and that had helped her to move on. If Callie could be that brave, he could too. Whatever difficulties stood ahead of them, they could be no match for love. He could face the risk of losing her if it meant he had a chance of keeping her.

Suddenly, from being sure about nothing, Ben was very sure about everything. Last Christmas had seemed like a bubble and the New Year a return to reality. But it was the other way around, and Christmas was the reality.

'I need you to do something…' He wondered if she'd guess what it was.

She moved in his arms, looking up at him. 'What's that? You'd like something to drink?'

'No.'

'Switch the gas fire on? It's getting a little chilly in here…' Callie grinned suddenly. She knew now, and she was just teasing him. Making the delicious anticipation last.

No.' Ben tightened his arm around her shoulders in case she took it into her head to move anyway.

'This?'

She moved closer, pausing before their lips finally met. The thought that this was so much more than he could ever deserve flitted briefly through his mind. And then there was no thought, just the feel of her arms around his neck and her body pressed close to his.

The kiss lasted until they were both breathless. And when she drew back, the look in Callie's eyes was almost as intoxicating.

'You're going to do that again?' Ben needed to be reminded that this wasn't all a dream.

'How soon?'

'Now…'

There was no doubt any more. When Callie kissed him again, he knew that this was a promise that wouldn't be broken.

'Please don't ever doubt me, Callie. I love you, and that's never going to change.'

'I love you too, Ben. That's never going to change either.'

Ben wound his arms around her. The here and now had just turned into for ever.

Ben's kiss was all she needed. Callie almost danced through the evening, cooking for them while he played with Riley, and Christmas carols echoed softly from the sound system. She'd taken the wreaths from the boxes of decorations and wound them around the balustrades at the edge of the mezzanine floor, the way they'd been last year.

He helped her bathe Riley and put her down to sleep, and then the evening was their own. Callie returned to the sofa, and Ben's arms, and he kissed her.

'There's something missing.'

'What's that? I'll fetch it immediately.'

He laughed. 'You'll need superpowers, if you're going to make it snow.'

Tonight it felt as if Callie really could conjure up snow. She could do anything she wanted to.

'I'll attend to the snow a bit later. I have something a little more pressing on my schedule.'

'Yeah? What's that?'

As if he didn't know. Callie kissed him, and Ben trailed kisses across her jaw. She felt his mouth on her neck and she shuddered with pleasure.

'You remember last year, lying in bed, with just the Christmas lights from the balcony...?'

She remembered. He'd traced the patterns that they made across her skin with his finger. And she'd watched the smooth ripple of light and shadow that had accompanied every move he'd made.

'Why do you suppose I put them up there?'

He chuckled. 'I'm not sure I can manage what came next...'

Callie put her finger over his lips. 'I doubt you can, but this'll be better. I'll arrange a few pillows to make you comfortable... You don't have to worry about anything, you'll be in the hands of a trained paramedic.'

He gave her a questioning look. 'That...could work.'

'Then...' she leaned in, whispering in his ear '... I'll rip your clothes off, and have my way with you. You might hurt a bit in the morning...'

He pulled her against his chest, holding her tight in his arms. 'That's very definitely going to work. Tomorrow can take care of itself.'

Just the two of them. Together. Callie had a feeling that everything was going to be just fine.

EPILOGUE

Two years later. Christmas Eve

THE PARTY FOR Ben and Callie's first wedding anniversary had wound down. Plates and glasses were stacked in the dishwasher, and after Riley had fallen asleep in her father's arms, Ben had put her to bed. He walked up to the mezzanine and found Callie, wearing a bright red cosy dressing gown and sitting cross-legged on the bed, stuffing Riley's Christmas stocking.

'That's very cute.' The dark blue felt stocking had an appliquéd Santa and his sleigh on it, along with sparkly snowflakes and shining golden stars.

'Isn't it just? Mum made a great job of it. Are you going to put it in her bedroom now?'

'I thought I'd give it an hour. Just to make sure she's fast asleep.'

Callie nodded, putting the stocking to one side. 'One year, Ben.'

'It couldn't have been a better one.' He took the small package out of his pocket, sitting down on the bed next to her. 'Happy anniversary, darling.'

She turned his gift in her hands, shaking it to see if it rattled. Her shining excitement made Ben smile. Then she undid the wrappings and opened the box, her hand flying to her mouth when she saw what it was.

'Ben! This isn't paper!'

'I couldn't wait another fifty-nine years to give you diamonds. I reckoned it would be good enough if I just wrapped them in paper.'

'They're beautiful, thank you.' She wrapped her arms around his neck, kissing him. 'So do you want me to try the earrings on or the paper?'

'Earrings first. If you don't like them we always have the wrapping paper to fall back on.' Ben watched as Callie took off her stud earrings and replaced them with his present. 'You look gorgeous.'

'Thank you. I love them. Would you like to come and see yours?'

'I have to come and see it?' Ben wondered what on earth Callie could have given him that he had to go to it, rather than it coming to him.

She took his hand and led him downstairs, tiptoeing past the open door of Riley's room and unlocking the door to the other side of the apartment. She'd been overseeing the last of the building works here while Ben had been busy with work. Every time he'd thought of coming in here to see the progress that was being made, Callie had headed him off, telling him she wanted him to wait until it was finished.

The faintest smell of new paint still hung in the air, and Callie led him past the new bedrooms and the playroom to the door that led to the new master bedroom. She made him close his eyes and then guided him into the room.

'You can look now.'

Ben opened his eyes and his breath caught suddenly. 'A wall? You've given me a wall! It looks fabulous...' The simplicity of the cream colour scheme set off the far wall perfectly. It had been sandblasted and sealed, something that Ben and Callie had talked about doing but had decided that they didn't have the funds.

'It's not just the wall.' She almost danced over to the far end of the room to a line of four photographs hung in plain, dark frames. The first was the one that Callie had taken of Ben that first Christmas at the fire station. Then Riley's first Christmas, followed by a photograph of Ben and Callie's wedding day. The fourth was one that Callie had taken of Ben and Riley together just a few days ago.

'We'll add to it. One photograph every year.'

She was hugging herself, grinning broadly at Ben's delight.

'There's plenty of space…'

'Then we'll have to make a lot of memories to fill it, won't we?'

A whole wall of Christmas memories. This was their future together, the one that they'd both taken a leap of faith to make possible.

'I love you, Callie.' However often he said it, those four words still seemed to take on a deeper, richer meaning every time. And Ben never tired of her reply.

'And I love you.'

He took her in his arms, holding her tight. 'It's been the best year, Callie. Your book deal, and the recognition of your work with burns patients.'

'And your new job. I hope you'll have a bit more time to spend at home now that the initiative's off the ground.'

'I will. Depend on it.' Ben had accepted a new job, heading up a task force to promote fire safety for the elderly. Callie been concerned that he might be taking it for her sake, and had insisted that he follow his own heart. But this was what he'd wanted to do, and the position had turned out to be even more challenging, and rewarding, than he'd hoped.

'I'll be wanting you here.' She stretched up,

kissing his cheek. 'We've just built three new bedrooms, and I can't fill them all on my own...'

A little brother or sister for Riley. If Ben could have predicted the one night of the year when that shared dream would come true, it would be this one. He smiled, gazing into her eyes.

'Are you ready for it, darling? Our future?'

She smiled up at him, and his heart almost burst with happiness. 'I can't wait...'

* * * * *

*If you enjoyed this story, check out
these other great reads from
Annie Claydon*

From Doctor to Princess?
Healed by the Single Dad Doc
Forbidden Night with the Duke
Saving Baby Amy

All available now!